Robert L. Preston

P L O T
THE

TO REPLACE THE CONSTITUTION

Published & Distributed
to Book Stores by

Hawkes Publications
4663 Rainbow Dr.,
Salt Lake City, Utah 84107
(801) 266-6200

Copyright 1972

by

Robert L. Preston

First Printing April 1972
Second Printing May 1972
Third Printing August 1972

Publisher & Bookstore Distributer

Hawkes Publications
4663 Rainbow Drive
Salt Lake City, Utah 84107

Dedicated to
Two of America's
Greatest Living Patriots

EZRA TAFT BENSON

W. CLEON SKOUSEN

ACKNOWLEDGEMENTS

The author is grateful to the writings of Ezra Taft Benson and W. Cleon Skousen for the knowledge gleaned from their work and the inspiration gained from the example of their patriotism. Appreciation is also expressed to Jewell Skonnard for her typesetting, to Linda Adams for her most valuable assistance with the manuscript, to Ben Skonnard for another great cover design and to John D. Hawkes, the kind of publisher every writer dreams of. A special thanks to those who give the most - my wife and family.

The Author

TABLE OF CONTENTS

TODAY EVERY AMERICAN IS ABOUT TO HAVE HIS PERSONAL RIGHTS AND FREEDOMS SWEPT AWAY AND TO BE REDUCED TO A SLAVE OF THE STATE. ALL OF THIS WILL HAPPEN SOON AS THE RESULT OF A VICIOUS PLOT BY ONE OF THE NATION'S MOST PRESTIGIOUS AND WEALTHY ORGANIZATIONS TO REPLACE THE UNITED STATES CONSTITUTION. THIS WILL BRING ABOUT ONE OF THE GREATEST TRAGEDIES IN THE HISTORY OF MANKIND, WITH RIOTING, MURDER, FAMINE, FIRE, PLUNDER AND PESTILENCE SWEEPING AMERICA!

Chapter One

THE CONSPIRACY

Every American who has watched television, read the newspapers or magazines of this country for the past ten years knows that a tremendous assault has been launched against our present way of life. Every conceivable excuse has been used to protest and riot—the draft, the war, college regulations, poverty, housing, racial differences—the list is as varied and endless as are human problems. There have been charges and countercharges of cover-ups and credibility gaps by the military, the government and the news media alike. Behind all of this smoke the average American has felt sure there must be some fire!

THE UNBELIEVABLE FIRE

Indeed there is a fire! It is such a clever fire, such a paradoxical fire, so well camouflaged behind the great billowing clouds of smoke, that most people have a difficult time believing the true nature of the fire once they are told what it is.

Let us consider a strange phenomenon that took place in England about 70 years ago. There we find three separate movements getting under way all at the same time, each of these movements being secretly united to the others by two common bonds, and yet each appearing to be a separate and distinct entity pursuing a different course. These three separate movements are the Foreign Relations Clubs, the Fabian Socialists, and the Communists. Uniting these three separate movements are a common goal of one-world government, and the financial backing of the richest and most wealthy and influential men in the world. Thus all three of these movements are merely three different prongs of a carefully coordinated and controlled attack by the richest men in the world to establish a one-world government, with them in charge.

Is this simply wild and unfounded conjecture on my part, created in a frantic attempt to put some sense into the nonsense of our disordered times, or can we prove it; can it be substantiated in fact? There is an old saying to the effect that if you give a thief enough rope he will hang himself with it. Fortunately, that is also true of those super-rich egotists who think they should run the whole world. Several of them have been so proud of their achievements in bringing the world closer to their dream of a one-world government with them in charge that they have been unable to resist the temptation to brag a little about their part in it. Though it has only been line upon line, over the course of seventy years, the bits and pieces begin to add up like the parts of a jigsaw puzzle, until at last the whole picture is clear. The fire behind the smoke is the conspiracy of the Super-Rich to rule the world.

THE DEVELOPMENT OF THE SUPER-RICH

Nearly two hundred years ago there lived a man in

Frankfurt, Germany, who was known as Mayer Ahmschel Bauer Rothschild. Mr. Rothschild, along with others of his time, discovered a very great principle. It was that whoever controlled the issue of credit and currency in a nation controlled the life of the nation. With an adequate flow of currency and credit, backed by sound reserves, a nation would grow and flourish. But when the credit and currency were withheld or the reserves were allowed to dwindle, the nation starved. Thus, those in control of the nation's credit and currency were, in reality, in charge of that nation; and by withdrawing credit and currency or by secretly removing the reserves, those in charge of the banking could depose kings, rulers, magistrates, premiers and presidents; for it was they who received the blame for the failing economy, not the banker. It appeared to the average person that when the economy failed, the banker suffered as well as anyone else; thus he was free of suspicion. But these bankers were wise enough to hold major interests in the banks that controlled the credit and currency of several nations. These were international bankers. They simply moved their wealth from one pocket to the next, and never lost a penny in the transaction. Mr. Rothschild, for example, had direct interests in the central banks (that is what the banks which control the credit and currency are called) of five different nations. So jealously did these bankers guard their financial position that for generations they would allow their children to marry only cousins. Gradually they began to marry into other international banking families. In the course of two hundred years, not more than a few dozen families have emerged as financial dynasties, arranged in a hierarchal order. (For more details, see the author's *How to Prepare for the Coming Crash.*)

THE CONSPIRACY SURFACES

From the year 1776 in Bavaria there was a secret conspiracy to rule the world. This conspiratorial group was known as the Illuminati. There is a great deal of evidence and information on the early workings of this organization. However, they soon ran into much opposition and were forced to become a super-secret organization. Little definite and reliable information is available after the early 1800's.

However, by the early 1900's those operating this conspiracy felt confident enough of their power to begin engineering, from behind the scenes, a disguised attack upon the established societies of the world. They began by aiding and abetting a movement that eventually came to be known as Communism. It is no coincidence that the goals and methods of Communism are identical to those of the Illuminati. From the very beginning, Karl Marx was supported by Frederik Engels, the wealthy German socialist. Even the *Communist Manifesto* was published largely through monies supplied by Clinton Roosevelt, a wealthy American who wrote a book denouncing the U.S. Constitution. Later, as a penniless Lenin brought his tiny band of followers to England, he was given financial aid by wealthy English and American capitalists. When he was ready to launch the Bolshevik Revolution in Russia, the capitalists of Germany, England and America all loaned or donated huge sums of money to finance the advance of Communism. In all, there is a record of several hundred million dollars flowing from the so-called hated capitalists to finance the triumph of Communism. (The author has completely documented this, and many other aspects of the conspiracy, in his book, *Wake-Up America, It's Later than You Think!*)

At the same time that the capitalists were financing the militants through Communism, they were encouraging a peaceful revolution of the world through a second group known as the Fabian-Socialists. This group was composed of the writers, the artists, playwrights, teachers, preachers, journalists, and all those who were willing to carry the banner of revolution. As with the Communists, their blood brothers, the Socialists taught doctrines and espoused causes that seemed to be directly contrary to the interests of the capitalists. Yet the capitalists continued, as though they were blind, to pour their money into the socialist causes. Even today the capitalists through their tax-free foundations continue to support all sorts of activities which are seemingly against them.

Also, simultaneously there emerged a third group. This group was the Foreign Relations Clubs, directly sponsored and supported by the Super-Rich. This group mingled into one group both the rich and the intellectuals. Here they paraded as public-spirited citizens willing to put the interests of state above their personal affairs, willing to donate their time and talents in a private organization which made a study of the nation's problems and which, after great expense and sacrifice, came up with a series of recommendations that the government should follow. It is strange how so many members of these private clubs found their way into all the top government posts. In the Nixon Administration, for example, the top 100 posts have gone to members of the Council on Foreign Relations, a private club, organized by the Rockefellers and the richest men in the country to influence the affairs of the nation. It is also strange that all of the recommendations of this private organization, com-posed of primarily the rich, have coincided and been in complete agreement with the goals announced by the Communist Party and the Fabian Socialists. But when we realize that all three of these movements are one and the same, that all are but parts of the Conspiracy by the Super-

Rich, that all are being financed and directed from the same source, it is not so strange after all.

THE INSIDE SPEAKS

Much of what has been just briefly outlined here, and covered more thoroughly in other works, would have remained forever in darkness had it not been for the irresistible temptation for those on the inside to brag a little. While in my other works I list these individuals and their revelations, here I will mention, briefly, only one.

One of those on the inside for many years, by his own admission, is Dr. Carroll Quigley, professor of history at Georgetown, and formerly of Princeton and Harvard, and author of several college texts on history. Dr. Quigley wrote a book of 1200 pages, which I believe was intended only for the eyes of potential converts to the Conspiracy. In this book, Dr. Quigley revealed that he felt these Super-Rich had developed such great power and the control of so many instruments of civilization that is—governments, corporations, newspapers, magazines, radio, television, colleges, churches, and foundations—that their grasp was unshakable. In addition to that he indicated that he felt their motives were good and that the Hope of the world was in cooperating with these men of ability, power and wealth and that the Tragedy of the future would lie in the great losses which would occur if we were to resist them. Thus came the title of his book, *Tragedy and Hope.* For an excellent review of this book I heartily endorse the great work by W. Cleon Skousen entitled, *The Naked Capitalist.* Also for further information I recommend Gary Allen's book, *None Dare Call It Conspiracy,* and my own *Wake-Up America, It's Later than You Think!*

CONQUERING AMERICA

When the Communists started out, they said they would conquer the whole world. No one in America took them seriously. However, by 1920 they had taken over all of Russia; by 1947 they had taken over all of Eastern Europe; by 1955 they had taken over all of China and by 1965 they had taken over Cuba, just 90 miles off the shores of the United States. The leaders of the Communist movement said that America would be the last to fall but that they would not have to attack; we would become so eroded that we would fall from within. The Conspiracy of the Super-Rich has so eroded this nation that we are now like a house that has been devoured by termites. The form and shape is still here, but the substance is gone. Just one good, well-placed blow could cause it to collapse.

For seventy years we have been infiltrated by the Conspiracy's deadly three-pronged attack. They have infiltrated our churches and have caused our ministers to turn away from God; over half of those in seminaries today deny the Divinity of Christ, and many teach that fornication and adultery are blessed in the sight of the Lord. They have infiltrated our schools; they have driven God from the classroom and replaced Him with sex education courses with the class project being to decide when to have premarital intercourse. They have caused millions of young people to believe that they are the descendants of an accidental creation—the end product of chance mutations—living without specific purpose and values, hopeless and lost, destroying themselves with drugs and the diseases of lust. They have destroyed our national sense of pride and self-respect through needless and evil wars designed not to be won; designed to eat up our young manhood, to fill our hearts with grief, and to turn us in upon ourselves lashing out in despair at the senseless hopelessness of it all. They have divided us up into groups one against another. We are no longer Americans, we have become black or white; young or old; woman or man; labor or management.

THE FINAL BLOW

Over the years, the Super-Rich have worked to gain control of the wealth of America just as they did in Europe. In 1913 with the founding of the Federal Reserve Banking System they achieved their goal. Since the establishment of that privately operated and owned banking system they have continued to gain an ever-tighter control over the financial affairs of this nation. Today they control every dollar in our country. By raising or lowering the Discount Interest Rate of the Federal Reserve, they can cause money to flow in or out of the economy, just as they wish. By regulating that interest rate, they can bring about a vast inflation of the currency and credit until the money becomes totally worthless if they want to. Or they can raise the interest rate so high that no one can get any money, and they can cause the entire economy to crash overnight. Such is the awesome power that resides in the hands of the bankers which own and control the Federal Reserve. Both Henry Cabot Lodge, Sr., and Charles Lindburg, Sr., were congressmen who saw what would happen if the Federal Reserve ever got their hands on our credit and currency. Both of these men stated that from that point on inflation and depressions would be scientifically created whenever the bankers wanted them.

Our money has become so overinflated and our gold reserves so depleted that the other nations of the world have forced us to devalue the dollar once and are pressuring us to devalue even more. The economy has become so totally artificial because of the manipulation of the Super-

Rich bankers that it is weak and sluggish, even with billions of dollars of credit and currency being poured into it.

Now all that needs to be done to totally destroy this once great and proud nation is to have the Super-Rich manipulators push the Discount Interest Rate up, and the nation will be on its economic knees. There will be little or no money in circulation. Foreclosures will be high. Loans will be called. Businesses will close. The unemployment rate will skyrocket. Food will disappear from the stores in the cities. People will starve. Riots will break out. Suddenly the nation will be in the midst of the worst national crisis it has ever faced. Meanwhile the Congress and the Executive Branch will seem to fall into deadlocked confusion. Nothing will seem to work. The situation will grow more grave and the American people more desperate by the hour. "Help us, oh please help us, my baby is dying because of a lack of food!" Everywhere the cry will go up for help. The news media will paint the most bleak and heartrending scenes anyone has ever witnessed.

ACCORDING TO PLAN

All of this will be according to plan. The Super-Rich have been planning this for a long time. They used the same technique to push this nation far away from strength, solvency, free enterprise and deep into controls, regulations, stiff taxes, and socialism with the deliberately rigged '29 crash. Now they plan to do it again. Of course, as in '29, it will look like an accident. And many a financial genius will confess to mistakes and miscalculations. "Sorry about that" will be the prevailing attitude. But the national crisis will be here, deep, and serious and treacherous; and it must be dealt with. That is the plan. For this time they plan to use the crisis as an excuse to give us a new constitution. The

Super-Rich and their stooges have been planning this for a long time, and now the stage is set.

THE REVELATION

In the fall of 1970 a very prestigious organization—The Center for the Study of Democratic Institutions, in Santa Barbara, California—published a new constitution for this nation. The Center was established in 1959 by the Fund for the Republic, which had been established by the Ford Foundation with a $15 million grant. As they published their version of a new constitution, they announced that they had been working on it for over six years and that they had engaged some of the most educated minds in the nation. Thus in the very sophisticated *Center Magazine* the inside leaders of the conspiracy were notified that the working guidelines for a new constitution for the nation were ready.

THE ADOPTION

Inspite of the many inroads, the many changes that have moved the nation down the road to socialism are still, after all, only temporary. The government still legally belongs to the people; and at any time, some courageous souls could rise up and take back their government and return it to what the Founding Fathers intended it to be. The Super-Rich do not like to think of all their work as being on a temporary basis. They are most anxious to make their mark a permanent one. Therefore they desperately want to get this new constitution adopted just as soon as possible in order to turn this nation permanently into a socialist dictatorship with them in charge.

PHASE ONE

When Mr. Tugwell, the prime author of this document,

was asked about how it would be possible to get this constitution adopted, he replied,

> . . . it could happen that the present system of government would prove so obstructive and would fail so abysmally to meet the needs of a continental people and a great power that general recognition of the crisis would occur. There might then be a redrafting of the basic law, and, if so, then it might be that this model we have worked over for a number of years might be taken into account." (p. 52, Vol. 3, No. 5, *The Center Magazine*)

What is being proposed here is that a national crisis will occur and this will establish the need for a new constitution. When we are aware that it is the Super-Rich that have funded the drafting of the new constitution, that it is the Super-Rich that have created a banking system that allows them to throw the nation into an economic depression at any moment, it becomes apparent that it would be very easy for the Super-Rich to plunge the nation into a crisis situation and push us into a new constitution when they have everything in readiness. An economic crisis is developing very rapidly and will probably culminate in an economic crash somewhere between early 1973 and early 1976. This will precipitate tremendous leverage on the people to accept a new constitution as the panacea of all their problems when it is offered to them by what appears to be all the good guys.

A CONTINENTAL PEOPLE

For the past several years the Super-Rich have been financing minority groups and leaders which have been causing all types of riots and civil disturbances. It is interesting to note that Mr. Tugwell refers to the people as being a continental people, whose needs will not be met. It will be the minority groups that will be the first to feel an economic crisis and will be hit the hardest and thus will be the very first to riot. Unknowingly these groups have been conditioned to riot by the Super-Rich so that when the deliberately arranged crash occurs they will riot automatically, creating the demands for the new constitution that will be used to enslave them.

PHASE ONE -- THE MILITANT MINORITIES

We feel that it would be grossly unfair to say that The Center has, in their published plan to replace the present constitution, openly advocated terrorism as a means of accomplishing it. What The Center has said concerning creating the demand for the new constitution is this:

> " . . . it could happen that the present system of government would prove so obstructive and would fail so abysmally to meet the needs of a continental people and a great power that general recognition of the crisis would occur." [1]

You will note that couched in their intellectual semantics they have said that the government could fail to meet the needs of minority groups and that a crisis would occur. Webster's Third New International Dictionary, 1968 edition, defines "continental" as meaning small or least part of something, such as minority groups. A common technique used by members of the left is to use words with little-known double meanings to convey one thing to the public and another to the inside members of their own group. As we examine the various crisis situations which have taken place thus far, we can easily see that they are caused by "a continental people"; that is, they are created by minority groups. Although many of the activities of these minority groups started out as nonviolent, they soon developed into very violent programs of hate and destruction.

22

These violent activities of minority groups not only can, as The Center indicated, create a national crisis, but they most certainly will, as that has long been the announced purpose of such violence. Max Stanford, U. S. leader of RAM, has stated:

> "The revolution will strike by night and spare none. Mass riots will occur in the day with the Afro-Americans blocking traffic, burning buildings, etc. Thousands of Afro-Americans will be in the street fighting; for they will know that this is it."[2]

Or as socialist scholar Martin Jay, teaching fellow at Harvard University, stated it:

> "Our movement is a movement which, in effect, is a total break with America."[3]

The Center indicates that the present government might not be able to cope with the problems raised by these minority groups. The Center knows, as does every socialist group in America, that it is deliberately intended that situations shall be continuously adjusted so that no solution is possible. The radical left has no intention of letting the "establishment" solve any of its problems. Said Dave Gilbert, a graduate student at the New School for Social Research in Manhattan, speaking at Princeton University to a special SDS conference:

> "We use the technique of demands, always pushing and pushing on through demands, to an end where they have to give in or fight against the revolution."[4]

In 1970 at the Sixth Annual Conference of Socialist Scholars, five "New Left" authors put forward a paper entitled "Towards a Socialist Strategy for the United States," in which they revealed their plan:

"to launch the social and cultural revolution on all fronts. This means desanctifying and putting into *crisis* all capitalist institutions and social relationships. . . . Thus, to carry through the revolution, it will be necessary to seize and dismantle the bourgeois state apparatus and to replace it by political forms which represent the working class."[5]

Though The Center has been careful to mask its plan for the adoption of a new constitution in the double entendre of Aesopian language, it is obvious from an examination of the statements of their fellow socialists that though the language may vary the plan and the meaning are the same. America is to be turned into a socialist-communist dictatorship by first using the minority groups to create demands, pressures, and finally such violence that the present form of government is made to seem ineffective and unworkable. A crisis is created wherein they plan to introduce as the only hope of solution, a new constitution.

A nation filled with confused and terrified citizens would be easily swayed to believe that all their problems will soon be over if they will just adopt this marvelous new document. This document will give the President broad new powers to cope with the situation and, at the same time, powers to enslave the people. A government powerful enough to save all the people is also powerful enough to enslave all the people.

PHASE TWO -- PLANTING THE SEED

The Center is not naive enough to believe that the constitution they have created will ever be adopted as written, either in part or in total. What they do know is that before something can be harvested a seed must first be planted. The new constitution as conceived by The Center is the seed. It is intended as food for thought among the intellectual and socialist community with the end result that a genuine new constitution will eventually emerge containing the concepts of socialism which they espouse. In an interview held at The Center with Mr. R. G. Tugwell, prime author of The Center's constitution, he stated, after outlining the national recognition of a crisis, that

> "There might then be a redrafting of a basic law (constitution) and, if so, then it might be that this model we have worked over for a number of years might be taken into account."[6]

Again in that same interview and in response to a question about the adoption of this version of a new constitution, Mr. Tugwell responded in part as follows:

> "This model is merely a collection of suggestions about what ought to go into a constitution adequate for the contemporary situation."[7]

In response to an earlier question, Mr. Tugwell had stated in part:

> "We never allowed ourselves to think that we were drafting a constitution that would ever be adopted as written by us."[8]

PREPARING THE WAY

There are three facts which clearly emerge from the responses of Mr. Tugwell concerning the adoption of The Center's constitution. The first is that no one needs to become overjoyed by the fact that when The Center published its constitution it was not inundated with tidal waves of acceptance. Those at The Center clearly understood there would at first be general resistance to the idea of a new constitution.

Note Mr. Tugwell's own comment concerning this fact:

"There is a great deal of resistance to doing anything about the Constitution at all."[9]

Even though forearmed with the knowledge that the public would be highly resistant to any changes, The Center spent six years of hard dedicated labor on producing a working model for a new constitution. No one works for six years, through thirty-seven revisions in the face of expected opposition if they are not very serious about the possibility that even though not adopted per se, it will "be taken into account."[10]

Americans in general and conservatives specifically like to analyze a problem, seek a solution and take a direct course of action. They tend to be impatient; they want to see action and they want it now. This makes it very difficult for them to be effective in resisting a movement of creeping socialism. When the socialist or communist conspirator makes a move which threatens the average conservative's way of life, he reacts with all of his adrenalin at full mast. But since nothing serious comes of this socialist-communist move at the moment, the adrenalin subsides and the average American goes back to sleep. The socialist-communist intellectuals are masters of psychology; they understand this phenomena very well. When they introduce a revolutionary concept, they already know the conservatives are going to react and go into full battle positions, tense and alert, waiting for the fight. They also know that no one can remain in that strained full-alert position for very long. Soon fatigue will begin to set in. The conservative American will begin to think his sudden show of strength has frightened off the socialist-communist advances. Or he will think that it was only a paper tiger, only a false alarm. Either way he will begin to relax his vigil. The conservative American is family and business oriented; he is a doer with many things he is anxious to get back to if the enemy does not want to come out and make a fight of it. All of this is well known to the intellectual socialist-communist community. Therefore they purposely test the water long before they actually expect to make their final move. Then by gradually introducing their ideas and concepts to the public over an extended period of time and from many different sources they are able to condition the public to accept them.

This concept was developed and perfected by Sidney and Beatrice Webb in the 1880's in London, who along with George Bernard Shaw were leaders of the Fabian Society, an organization dedicated to converting the world to a one-world socialist government. This concept was given the title of "The Doctrine of the Inevitability of Gradualness."

When we examine the tremendous inroads socialism has made in the United States during the past forty years, we can easily see the effectiveness of this doctrine. Certainly The Center is not ignorant of this doctrine and had this in mind when they authored their version of a new constitution.

TAKEN INTO ACCOUNT

The second fact that clearly emerges from a study of this work by The Center is that they fully expect their work " . . . to be taken into account"; that is, they seriously expect their ideas to be carefully considered when a new constitution is drafted. Although they have masqueraded the production of this new constitution as an internal exercise for "sharpening our discussions and our thinking about what a constitution should be and do," it is obvious that it is far more than this.

Normally, *The Center Magazine* consists of numerous articles and papers on a great variety of socialistic thought; however, so much value was placed upon this little exercise that an entire issue of their magazine was devoted to it from cover to cover. The editor of *The Center Magazine,* John Cogley, thought so much of this little exercise that he devoted his editorial space to describing the value of what had been done and at one point had this to say:

> "It is the editor's judgment that in its short history this magazine has not published anything of more current significance or lasting interest than this xxxvii version of the Tugwell draft."[11]

This distinguished magazine has a reading audience which consists of members of the Supreme Court as well as many lower courts, many members of both houses of Congress, leading members of the executive branch of the Federal government as well as top officials in state and local governments throughout the nation, leading members of the clergy, news media and of course, the educational fraternity. When the editor of such a highly influential publication is willing, even anxious, to devote his entire issue to covering something which he declares to be ". . . of more current significance or lasting importance . . ." than anything previously published, he is either taking an awful slap at his previous contributors or he feels that he has something of more than ordinary value.

Obviously, the excuse that the creation of this constitution was merely an internal exercise for sharpening their own thinking is a very thin veneer to cover their desire to see the United States adopt a new constitution that would make this nation over to their own liking.

The statement that the Tugwell draft is of "current significance" causes one to wonder what is so significant about it since the original constitution has served the nation so well for so many years. It would seem that the most significant thing about it is that it launches a very serious effort to give the United States a new constitution, a constitution created by a group of intellectual socialists who dream of uniting the world under the banner of state control and ownership. Although it is obvious that The Center has no illusions about their version of the constitution being adopted as written by them, it is equally obvious that they seriously think the time is quite near when a new constitution will be adopted by this nation, and they intend their ideas to be of "current significance." If there is any doubt in your mind as to how much impact The Center expects this new constitution to have, it should be dispelled by the following quote:

> "We are often surprised ourselves by the influence a quiet discussion held in Santa Barbara later has on the larger world. Thoughts originally put forth at The Center and later published in *The Center Magazine* frequently find their way into classrooms, pulpits, mass-circulation publications, radio and television discussion programs, and professional meetings. Readers of *The Center Magazine* and of our other publications have carried the word throughout the world."[12]

From tiny seeds nocuous weeds do grow. The seed has now been planted, planted in the fertile soil of a revolutionary-minded age. Now it will be nurtured and tended in "classrooms, pulpits, mass-circulation publications, radio and television discussion programs, and professional meetings." Slowly, ever so slowly, it will begin to grow and take root in the hearts and minds of America's socialist revolutionaries. Gradually it will begin to emerge on the public scene, first as only a thought for consideration, a mental exercise. Then within a very short span of time we shall suddenly realize that the idea is favorably being talked about everywhere. Before you will be able to realize it, you will be voting on it.

PLANNED FROM THE BEGINNING

The third fact that emerges from a study of The Center's revelations concerning their new constitution is that writing it was not an incidental program thrown in at random along the way: rather it was planned for from the beginning. In fact, Robert M. Hutchins, Chairman, has written in an open letter to Center members that from the earliest meetings to organize The Center and consider the issues to be studied

". . . the Constitution of the United States was a recurring theme."[13]

Mr. Hutchins then goes on to point out that the present constitution does not mention a whole host of modern conditions including "the organization of the world," [14] obviously a serious oversight on the part of the Founding Fathers. It is interesting to note that as the organizers met to consider the issues,

"The consultants did not attempt to settle the question whether the United States needs a new constitution. They did agree that the effort to frame one would be a worthwhile undertaking for the Center for the Study of Democratic Institutions: it would bring all the interests of the Center into focus . . ."[15]

It would appear that there really was no question as to whether the United States needed a new constitution. A nation which had a constitution which was so outdated that it "had become largely a myth and myths are easily exposed"[16]

is obviously in need of a new constitution. Therefore, it seems that The Center has decided that it ". . . would be a worthwhile undertaking . . ."[17] for them to come to the aid of their country with a wonderful new socialist constitution.

The Center Magazine editor, John Cogley, states in his editorial comments that:

> "those who believe that the United States needs a new constitution will find here a starting point for their own model-making."[18]

Apparently Mr. Cogley believes that there are others who share The Center's belief that the United States needs a new constitution.

In at least three separate places the various spokesmen for The Center have stated that one of the prime purposes of drafting this working model of a new constitution was to bring into focus all of The Center's discussions and activities. According to the dictionary, "focus" means a convergence to a central point. Therefore, it would appear that central to everything said or done at The Center has been the concept that the United States needs a new constitution and that The Center should concentrate all of its power and resources into bringing it about. This should serve as a warning to every American that loves his freedoms. For when an organization with the financing, the staff and the influence The Center has sets out to give the nation a new constitution, you had better believe that it very well may do it.

Chapter Two

THE CONSPIRATORS

From the dawn of recorded time man has been attempting to develop a system of government that would eliminate such problems as poverty, prejudice, partiality before the law, hunger, disease, housing, and a list as long as the problems of man. Over the centuries there has gradually emerged a great wealth of knowledge born out of experience.

In the year of 1776 on the continent of North America there gathered together a group of men dedicated to setting up just such a government based upon the wisdom of history. During the next two hundred years the government those men founded protected the rights of more diverse peoples, races, creeds, colors, and religions than had any other government known to man. The results of protecting those rights was phenomenal. Men of all types and backgrounds soon began to enjoy the opportunity of freedom and its precious fruits. Wealth, comfort, conveniences, luxuries, and astounding material achievements began to be common place among the people of the land.

But, as always, not all could enjoy the fruits of freedom in a great nation. There were those of power and influence who used their wealth and influence to buy their way around the just laws of the land. They escaped the earthly accounting for every crime, both moral and legal. Those who earned millions influenced laws, causing them to pay little or nothing in taxes to support the government which had made their vast fortunes possible, while the poor wage earner with a family had a large share of his income forcibly removed from his pay in advance. Those of minority racial backgrounds were often the target of social and legal injustices that were designed to hold them back, to keep them from enjoying the full freedoms of the land. The results were pockets of ignorance, poverty, hunger, disease, and crime. Such conditions are a cancer that eat away at a government, at a society and a nation of people. Either the condition must be cured or it will destroy the body of the nation in which it resides.

The question is not just one of whether the conditions of injustice must be cured, but one of "How is the best way to cure them?" To those great men who risked everything to found this nation the best way to cure these ills was in a climate of responsible freedom. It was their belief that man was the product of a Divine Source, a Creator that had endowed him with certain inalienable rights. But beyond being endowed by the Creator with inalienable rights they also believed that man had been endowed with the power of mind and spirit to live justly, to live responsibly. This concept permeated every fiber of the national life, churches, public schools, colleges, books, magazines, newspapers, business and financial institutions. The concept of a responsible character created by self-will among the adults and molded into the child by his early environment forged a nation with a high moral character. This concept came to be known as the "Protestant" or "Judeo-Christian Ethic," as it was based upon the principles of Christianity as understood by the early religious settlers.

As this ethic grew and flourished, the raw and lawless frontier was replaced by civilization. Vigilantes, kangaroo courts, posses, and hanging parties were replaced by lawyers, judges and juries; and the rights of the accused gradually came to be protected, but not at the expense of the rights of society or the victimized. Schools and churches pushed out the saloons and brothels. America grew from a raw untamed wilderness, a wild and lawless frontier to become the most highly civilized nation on the face of this earth — not by the use of laws or force but by the use of the greatest power on earth, the responsibility of good character in a free human being.

Now we are at a crossroad in the history of mankind. A decision is being forced upon this nation and in turn the world. That decision is "shall we go on into the future and solve our problems with the responsibility of good character in individual freedom, or shall we go into the future and solve our problems with government regulations?"

Since the beginning there have been those who have, for one reason or another, thought that they could more perfectly run society. Given the power to control the lives of the people, they have believed that they could more perfectly eliminate the evils of the world. Given sufficient control to direct the lives of men and women and children, given the power to regulate the affairs of industry and economics, given the power to regulate affairs of state, given the power to regulate life as though they were God, they have believed they could create utopia. All we the people have to do to find out is to give to them all power and control over every aspect of our lives.

Today we have in the United States, government of the people, by the people and for the people. That the government does not always function for the people is because we the people have not always been as attentive to our personal civic responsibilities as we should be and not because the system of government is evil within itself. Even though the government may have strayed far from its intended path of allowing the maximum of personal freedom with a minimum of interference, still, as long as the Constitution remains intact, we the people have it within our power to rise up and take our freedoms back again. The government as it is now structured by the Constitution is responsive to the will of the people. When the people become sluggish and lackadaisical, the government becomes sluggish and lackadaisical as well, not because it is bad but because it is responsive to the will of the people. Still the people can be aroused to their duties and responsibilities, and once again the government will assume its rightful duties and responsibilities to the people.

Those who would play a role that even God does not take upon Himself, would take away our freedoms, regulating and controlling every aspect of our lives, are aware that we the people can rise up at any moment and take complete control of our government. This is very disconcerting to those who believe they know what is best for the world and have worked so long and hard to bring it to pass. Their greatest sense of insecurity and hence their greatest concern is in the power of the people through the present form of constitutional government. They realize that in order for their work to have any sense of permanence, any real hope of success, they must first take away the right of the people to control the government.

Thus it is that we now find the beginning of a movement to scrap the present Constitution and replace it with another which would eventually invest all power into the hands of those relative few who think they know what is best for all the world. A brief examination of the life and works of some of the central figures in the production of this working model for a new constitution will reveal that they are indeed among those who think they know what is best for the rest of us.

THE FORD FOUNDATION

Because it was primarily due to the financial generosity of the Ford Foundation that the new constitution was written, we shall begin with an examination of the Foundation and its associates. Due to the very stringent laws of inheritance which had been passed by the United States, it was not possible upon the death of Henry Ford, Sr., for the family to pay the large taxes required and still retain the family's ownership of the business. It would necessitate selling the largest portion of the business or giving it away in order to avoid the huge tax that would be required. Since Mr. Ford had long held an intense dislike for Wall Street financiers, it was his fervent wish to avoid selling any stock in his company that might fall into the hands of the Wall Street tycoons. It was therefore decided to establish the Ford Foundation and transfer between eighty-eight and ninety per cent of the stock in nonvoting shares to the Foundation. While only owning between ten and twelve per cent of the business themselves, the family still retained control of the business because theirs was the only voting stock. In addition to this, members of the family held various positions within the company and could pay themselves such large salaries as to insure that no profits would be left to divide among the stockholders. Inasmuch as approximately ninety per cent of the stock was being held by the Foundation, it would be to the family's advantage to keep their salaries high enough to keep the Ford Motor Company operating almost at cost.

Acting as a board of trustees for the Ford Foundation were members of the Ford family, trusted friends and associates. So long as Henry and Edsel were alive, the family retained control of the Foundation and its activities. However, upon their death, the hired administrators began to emerge with more and more control and the trustees with less and less. By 1948 Paul G. Hoffman had been appointed President of the Foundation, and the work of the Foundation took a sudden and sharp turn to the left. There immediately began a reorganization and redirection of the Foundation's work. A special committee was appointed to determine the directions the Foundation should take. The committee's results have been well reviewed by the well-known columnist Raymond Moley as follows:

> "[the committee was] composed of a lawyer, H. Rowan Gaither, Jr., now president of the foundation; a doctor; a school administrator; and five professors. None of these was experienced in foundation work. It could hardly be called a coincidence that the five areas which they recommended for the foundation correspond, to a degree, to the academic departments in which the professors had been teaching. The plan substantially ruled out medical research public health, and natural science on the vague ground that 'progress toward democratic goals are today social rather than physical.' 'Democratic goals' are nowhere defined."[1]

The five areas in which "Democratic goals" were to be pursued are the establishment of peace, the strengthening of democracy, the strengthening of the economy, education in a democratic society, and individual behavior and human relations.

In 1949 a special report had been prepared under the direction of Mr. Hoffman; it was presented to and accepted by the trustees. It stated in part that

> "Individual members of the Board of Trustees should not seek to decide the technical questions involved in particular applications and projects. Nothing would more certainly destroy the effectiveness of a foundation. On the contrary, the Trustees will be most surely able to control the main lines of policy of the Foundation, and the contribution it will make to human welfare, if they give the Presi-

dent and the officers considerable freedom in developing the program, while they avoid influencing [even by indirection] the conduct of projects to which the Foundation has granted funds."[2]

Thus did the Board of Trustees to a very large extent turn over the control to the hired hands.

SUPPORTING COMMUNIST CAUSES

At this point the Ford Foundation embarked on a wide ranging dispensation of funds to a variety of causes, all of which were to the left of center and had to do with remolding the thinking process of the American people to accept the idea of a complex world which required the deft manipulations of a hierarchy of dedicated souls on behalf of all the rest of us. To those associated with the Foundation, the word "Communism" seemed to hold a special charisma that they could not resist. They not only came to the aid of communist causes but defended and championed them. An example of their befriending the communist cause is the attitude expressed by the Foundation when giving grants in aid to the American Friends Service Committee in 1951 and 1952. They stated that the Foundation "felt that the American Friends Service Committee had demonstrated over a long period its capacity to deal effectively with many of the economic, social and educational conditions that lead to international tensions."

As an example of the AFSC's having great capacity to deal effectively with problems of world tension we might cite the fact that while America was at war with North Vietnam — with our American boys being killed and wounded daily, others rotting with no medical aid, little food and clothing and subjected to barbaric tortures in North Vietnam prison camps — the AFSC took boatloads of foods and supplies to the North Vietnamese to aid their war effort. The

39

AFSC began in 1950 with President Truman and has continued down to the present time to work for full diplomatic recognition of Red China, with great success, it might be added, on the grounds that "by treating Communist China as an enemy and by refusing to recognize her, we are isolating ourselves." The AFSC have been spouting that line for more than twenty years. It does seem to be a strange bit of logic that allows the AFSC to call someone who has sworn to destroy you, to bury you, to erode you until you fall into their hands and they completely take you over, a friend. It does seem strange to call not giving aid and succor to those that have sworn to conquer you, self-isolation; but nonetheless that is the reasoning and logic of the AFSC — somehow I gain the distinct impression that they may also be the enemy.

In justifying this grant to such a befriender of communism, the Foundation had these noble words to say on the subject:

> "It is surprising that we have not been able to understand the situation in Asia because Americans should be peculiarly able to comprehend the meaning of revolution. Our own independence was achieved through a revolution, and we have traditionally sympathized with the determined attempts of other people to win national independence and higher standards of living. The current revolution in Asia is a similar movement, whatever its present association with Soviet Communism."[3]

It is difficult to believe, I know, but that really is the Ford Foundation speaking. They seem to have forgotten their history lessons. When we fought, it was for freedom *from* a foreign power. Now they want to enslave independent nations *to* a foreign power and call it the same thing as the American Revolution. And these are the same people, exactly the same people, who are behind the writing of the suggested new constitution. These are the people who believe that they can do better for us than we can do for ourselves.

Now let's keep in mind that at the time the preceding statements were made by the Ford Foundation on behalf of the American Friends Service Committee and Communism, the President was Paul G. Hoffman and his number one assistant at fifty thousand dollars a year was Robert M. Hutchins. At the time the new constitution project was undertaken by The Center for the Study of Democratic Institutions, the same Paul G. Hoffman was the Chairman of the Board, and Robert M. Hutchins was President of The Center. At the time of the publication of the new constitution six years later, Mr. Hoffman had moved up to be the Honorary Chairman of the Board and Mr. Hutchins was Chairman of the Board, as well as the Chairman of the Senior Fellows of The Center.

As we continue to examine the lives and works of the central figures of this new constitution, we see a thread of continuity that runs through it all — a dedication to the concept that a united world government based upon the principles of communist-socialism is their main objective.

There is an old saying that "birds of a feather flock together." As we examine the lives of those involved in the production of The Center's new constitution, we see this overwhelmingly born out. All of the key figures previously have been involved in overlapping activities designed to bring about a one-world communist-socialist government. As we review some of their previous activities, it becomes very apparent that they are not interested in preserving the sovereignty of the nation or the individual. In the name of doing good for all they would enslave us all, for what is government control and regulation of every aspect of our lives but slavery?

41

PAUL G. HOFFMAN

Beginning in 1911, at the age of twenty, Mr. Hoffman proceeded to build an automobile dealership for the Studebaker Company to such heights that by 1924, at the age of thirty-three, his business volume was in excess of seven million dollars a year. His success was so great that in 1925 he was offered the vice-presidency in charge of sales for the Studebaker Corp. Within a few years the company went into receivership due to bad management. One of the receivers was Paul Hoffman. Because of his brilliant management, the company was soon back on its feet, and Mr. Hoffman was installed as the President of the company.

In 1942 he joined with several other men to form the Committee for Economic Development, an offshoot of the Council on Foreign Relations, of which he was also a member. Not only did Mr. Hoffman become the Chairman of the Board of the C.E.D., but he also served on the staff of its research division. This has special significance because of the three other members of the staff — Theodore Yntema, Beardsley Ruml, and Thomas W. Lamont, two of which were selected from the faculty of the University of Chicago, whose President at that time, strangely enough, was Robert M. Hutchins. Theodore Yntema, a University of Chicago faculty member, was selected to be the director of the C.E.D.'s research division.

Another member was Beardsley Ruml, formerly the University of Chicago Dean of the Department of Social Sciences. Mr. Ruml was also the man responsible for the creation of the tax plan that allows the government to withdraw your income tax from your salary each payday before you get it. His plan also shifted the heaviest burden of taxation onto the lower income groups. He traveled extensively in Russia during the Lenin and Stalin years and was quite fond of wearing Russian peasant blouses. He was also the originator of the domestic allotment plan, the basis for the New Deal farm program, and was Chairman of the New York Federal Reserve Bank.

Rounding out the staff was Thomas W. Lamont, chief advisor and assistant to the great financial giant J. P. Morgan. He has been referred to as one of the most powerful men on both sides of the Atlantic because of his deep financial ties with the international banking world. He was heavily involved with financial deals of all types during both world wars with interests both at home and abroad and involving both private and government contracts. Long interested in political economics, he endowed Harvard University with a five hundred thousand dollar grant to establish a professorship of political economics which he personally controlled. He became a close advisor to both Presidents Wilson and Hoover and spent much time in Washington conferring with them, and when not there in person it was said that he kept the phone lines hot to the White House. He was an advocate of a United States of Europe and was one of the key designers of The League of Nations, forerunner to the United Nations. His son, Corliss, has been an outspoken author of left-wing activities and causes and at one time was Chairman of Friends of the Soviet Union and a member of the National Council of American-Soviet Friendship. When in January, 1946, Corliss Lamont refused to cooperate with the House Un-American Activities Committee which was investigating these organizations, he was cited for contempt of Congress on June 26, 1946, and denounced as "probably the most persistent propagandist for the Soviet Union to be found anywhere in the United States."[4] Still when Thomas Lamont remade "his will on Jan. 6, 1948, Corliss L. Lamont remained in it as co-heir to his father's fortune of scores of millions of dollars."[5]

These two brief resumes of associates of Mr. Hoffman are sufficient to indicate the internationalist, socialist ties and associations that intertwined their lives and united them in a common cause.

Rising out of these associations during the 1940's was the invitation to assume the leadership of the Ford Foundation and later of the fifteen million dollar Fund for the Republic. One of the many communist-centered activities the Fund financed under his direction was "a study of the 'influence of Communism in contemporary America.' A key member of the staff for this study was Earl Browder, long-time National Secretary of the Communist Party."[6] As a delegate to the United Nations in 1956 and 1957 he suggested setting up a United Nations Special Fund, which was accomplished Jan. 1, 1959. Mr. Hoffman was appointed the Managing Director of the Fund and has remained so continuously, no doubt because he is doing such a good job. For example, according to Representative Durwood Hall (R-Mo.) in 1959, the United States contributed $10,300,000 to the Fund, compared to the combined communist-bloc contribution of $1,593,000. By 1963 Mr. Hoffman had been able to engineer the United States' contribution up to $29 million while the entire communist-bloc contribution had remained at a lowly $1,685,000. What is especially interesting is that none of this money is spent within the United States, but it is dispersed on various projects among some 150 countries throughout the world, many of which are communist countries. All of the contributing communist nations which do give, give with the restriction that not more than 20 to 25 per cent of their contribution may be spent by the Fund outside the communist-bloc. As an example of how this program has worked at the expense of the American taxpayer to build up the communist countries, we will note that over a five-year period Yugoslavia contributed a total of $957,000 and over the same period received in aid from the Fund a total of $2,627,000. Even while not recognizing Cuba, an enemy in fact that was pointing nuclear missiles at the U. S., we contributed in 1961-62 some 40 per cent of the cost of a $1,157,600 grant-in-aid to Castro's agricultural program. Even though there was an official protest filed with the U.N. by the U. S. delegation objecting to the use of these taxpayer funds going to communist Cuba, on Feb. 13, 1963, Mr. Paul Hoffman announced that the grant was going to be made anyway. Another example of Mr. Hoffman's benefaction to the communist-bloc with U. S. money is the authorization of a project in communist Yugoslavia labeled "Nuclear Research and Training in Agriculture" . . . in agriculture? Well, that is what the man said. Among the many ultra-socialist-communist groups he has belonged to and supported have been such beauties as Americans United for World Government.

Obviously Mr. Hoffman does not fall into the category of a Jefferson, or Franklin, or Adams, and is not what I would call the ideal type to be influencing the writing of a new constitution for the United States of America.

ROBERT M. HUTCHINS

Not only does Mr. Hutchins play an important role as chief administrator at The Center where the new constitution was drafted, but he also played an important role as a principal contributor, as we may discern from the following remarks by Mr. Tugwell, the prime author of the constitution:

> "But the person in the group who knows most about this kind of enterprise and who has followed the Supreme Court's interpretation of the Constitution for many years is Robert Hutchins. I always felt that his evaluation of the model would be the one that would probably come closest to being the kind of thing we wanted to achieve."[7]

Since Mr. Hutchins' ideas were going to "come closest" to the kind of constitution The Center wanted to produce, it would be interesting to know the kind of thoughts and feelings Mr. Hutchins has that are going to influence such an important document as a new constitution for the United States.

Mr. Hutchins began his career as an educator in 1925, teaching at the Yale Law School; by 1928, at the age of twenty-nine, he was the Dean of the school. The following year, at the age of thirty, he became President of the University of Chicago. There he began revolutionizing the teaching programs of all departments by integrating into each of them a broad liberal social studies curriculum. Through this social studies program he was able to interject liberal social concepts into every study program from biological science to engineering. Many professors resigned in disgust, but they were easily replaced by others far more sympathetic to the liberal-social ideas Mr. Hutchins was determined to implant in the minds of the students at the University of Chicago. By 1945 he had also become the University's first Chancellor. While in that position, he became an editor for Encyclopedia Britannica and editor-in-chief for the Great Books of the Western World of which he was one of the main sponsors and promoters. In 1945 he also became the President of an organization entitled Committee to Form a World Constitution, a position which he has held continuously since that time.

Obviously Mr. Hutchins is interested in a new constitution for the United States as a groundwork to ease us into a constitution for world government. He was one of the originators of the tactic to scare the nation into cooperation with the communist nations of the world on the grounds that to do otherwise might lead to a nuclear holocaust of such tragic proportions as to make it wiser to yield our government and national sovereignty over to a socialist-communist world government. He stated this belief on August 12, 1945, at a University of Chicago Round Table Discussion.

In 1951 he was associate director of the Ford Foundation where he befriended socialist-communist causes of every ilk. In 1954 he was appointed President of the newly formed Fund for the Republic and in 1959 was also appointed President of its offshoot, the Center for the Study of Democratic Institutions.

The Encyclopedia Britannica states,

"In the 1960 annual report of the fund and of its Center for the Study of Democratic Institutions, Hutchins said that man must try to discover another basis for rational discussion since great technological and political changes had made obsolete many vital ideas of the past such as 'universal suffrage' and 'free enterprise.'"[8]

Obviously, anyone who has come to the point that he thinks the right of free Americans to vote and engage in business is obsolete is a very dangerous man to be influencing the drafting of a new constitution for the United States. It is apparent from his actions, his associations and his statements that he believes wholeheartedly in a socialist-communist dictatorship that would eliminate the right of the average person to vote and would of course do away with all of the advantages of a free-enterprise system. It is Mr. Hutchins' desire to see that all men, except the chosen and enlightened few, live on a guaranteed, truly minimum annual wage. To Mr. Hutchins the secret of Utopia as he would envision it is to reduce the average man and woman to nothing more than an ant in a hill, to provide for their needs as a race horse owner would provide for his horse and allow them about the same amount of freedom and opportunity.

Mr. Hutchins is hardly of the same calibre or school of thought as that of Jefferson, Franklin, and Adams, but is definitely in a class with Marx, Lenin, and Stalin. A man that would declare the communist enslavement of millions of people in Asia, through the murder and torture of millions— the same thing as the American Revolution is hardly the man to be entrusted with the delicate and sensitive responsibility of creating governments for millions of free Americans.

SCOTT BUCHANAN

In response to a question about the influences he had received in preparing his draft of a new constitution, Mr. Tugwell responded,

> "I might say that the criticisms I got from the late Scott Buchanan were general and quite profound. He and I had many long discussions."[9]

While we may never know the exact content of those "many long discussions," we may easily glean the nature of them by examining the life and works of Mr. Buchanan. As with Robert Hutchins, Scott Buchanan was a prodigy in the field of college administration. He had been a Rhodes scholar at Oxford in England where his studies of Plato's philosophies had a great influence on his philosophies of life. The significance of the preceding statement will emerge with great force later in the book as we deal with the relationship of Plato, John Ruskin, and Cecil Rhodes. However, it will be sufficient to note at this point that Rhodes scholars at Oxford were specifically taught a socialistic philosophy of life as it was revealed by Plato in his book, *The Republic.* After returning to America, he became a college professor and soon thereafter he became a college administrator. His book *Possibility* was lauded by the arch-liberal educator John Dewey as "having many seeds of thought for intellectual discussions."

In 1936 at the request of Robert Hutchins, he became Chairman of the Liberal Arts Committee for the University of Chicago. He helped to develop the "Great Books" program and when he subsequently became Dean of St. John's College in Annapolis in the fall of 1937, he carried that program with him. He remained in that post until 1947 when he resigned to pursue his interest in writing. From 1948 through 1958 he served as consultant, trustee and secretary of the Foundation for World Government. In 1957, again at the request of Robert Hutchins, he became a consultant to the Fund for the Republic and a fellow at The Center for the Study of Democratic Institutions where he remained until the death of his body in 1968. Once again we see the crossing of lives at the University of Chicago and the preoccupation with the formation of a world government through overt action.

REXFORD GUY TUGWELL

Last but not least we come to the prime author of the new constitution, Mr. Rexford Guy Tugwell. As young Tugwell grew up working between school terms on routine labor jobs, he became deeply disturbed by the poverty and distressing conditions of many of the minority groups with which he shared this type of work. He felt that someone ought to do something about their condition. As the years passed and his education accumulated, he began to formulate the idea that more government planning and control could provide more and better jobs with a more even distribution of the wealth of the nation. During his late high school and early college years he held jobs as a reporter for various small newspapers. After receiving his master's degree he became a college instructor. Upon receiving his doctorate, he began a seventeen year teaching career at Columbia University, rising through the ranks from instructor to assistant, to associate, to full professor in economics. During this period he turned out a series of books expounding his concepts of government planning and control for the benefit of society rather than having freedom for the benefit of the individual.

In 1927 as a member of the first American Trade Union Delegation to the Soviet Union, he extensively toured Russia and reinforced his ideas on government control and planning. Upon his return he co-authored a chapter on Russian agriculture in the book *Soviet Russia in the Second Decade.* His co-authors were communist Robert W. Dunn and fellow traveler Stuart Chase. It was Stuart Chase's book entitled *New Deal* that inspired F.D.R. to call his program by that name. A brief quote from the book will give you some insight into the philosophy of the men Tugwell chose to associate with:

> "Best of all, the new regime would have the clearest idea of what an economic system was for. The sixteen methods of becoming wealthy would be proscribed [punished] – by firing squad if necessary – ceasing to plague and disrupt the orderly processes of production and distribution. The whole vicious pecuniary complex would collapse as it has in Russia. Money-making as a career would no more occur to a respectable young man than burglary, forgery or embezzlement." [10]

Anyone caught making money would be punished if they had their way, by firing squad if necessary, and our whole financial system would fold just as it has in Russia. Now wouldn't that be wonderful. What a Utopia we would have — poor medical care, no housing, no cars, not enough food to buy even if we had the money to buy it. It is interesting to note that while these men decry profits and money-making, all of them have had positions where they have been personally paid salaries ranging from twenty to in excess of fifty thousand dollars per year, and none of them have taken liberally of their means to solve the problems of the down-trodden they profess to be interested in helping. Yet if they have their way, you and I will be held to a common level with all other men except, of course, them, the ruling class.

Beginning in 1928 Tugwell became involved in politics as a vehicle to put his ideas into practice. First he campaigned for the Socialist Party ticket and Norman Thomas, but by 1932 had swung to the Democratic ticket as a more logical chance of putting his ideas to work and supported Roosevelt. In 1933 he became the chief assistant to Henry Wallace in the Department of Agriculture. It is interesting to note that as he left Columbia University, Tugwell coined the following verse to describe the revolution he forthwith intended to inflict upon America:

"I am sick of propertied czars.
I have dreamed my great dreams of their passing.
I have gathered my tools and my charts.
My plans are finished and practical.
I shall role up my sleeves —
              and make America over."11

In order to sharpen his socialist ideas even more, Dr. Tugwell also took a teaching post at the Rand School of Social Science, along with his associate in writing on Russian agriculture, Stuart Chase, the New Dealer. *(Rand School Bulletin, 1934-35).* At the Rand School Tugwell had the opportunity to rub shoulders with ideas coming directly from the London Fabian Society, the wellspring of the plot to establish a world socialist government. As a result of these influences, Tugwell moved into government circles with zeal and ideas that transformed America from the land of the free to the land of the socialized. To say that Tugwell's influence in the Roosevelt administration was extensive is to put it mildly. Rose L. Martin tells it this way in her great documentary work *Fabian Freeway.*

> "There was little in the application of the early New Deal in which Tugwell did not have a finger. Besides abetting Wallace in a forlorn attempt to transform abundance into scarcity by ploughing under crops and killing suckling pigs, Tugwell also sat on the Housing Board, the Surplus Relief Administration, the Public Works Board, the President's Commercial Policy Committee, and other newly created bodies. He fathered the thought, seconded by the President's Commercial Policy Committee, of grading all industry according to their efficiency and utility and denying tariff protection to those judged a 'burden' on the United States.
>
> It was Tugwell who proposed that consumers be represented, in addition to labor unions and employers, on the twenty-seven industry boards to set up the National Recovery Act. The object of this seemingly benevolent move was to cut prices and profits, while increasing wages — a prelude to the disappearance of the profit system, which a number of New Dealers believed to be close at hand." [12]

While Tugwell was slaving away as Under-Secretary of Agriculture, doing his very best to socialize America, he had the help of some very able men, also working in that department. The first head of the Agricultural Adjustment Administration, George N. Peek, states:

> "A plague of young lawyers settled on Washington; in the legal division were formed the plans which eventually turned the AAA from a device to aid the farmers to a device to

introduce the collectivist system of agriculture into this country." 13

They were an elite group that had fallen under the influence and direction of Harold Ware, the first American Secret Soviet Agent. Ware was an agriculture expert and had worked for the government as a dollar-a-year man from the year 1925 through 1932, and knew his way around the Department of Agriculture. His assignment was to set up a communist cell in the Department of Agriculture; and that is exactly what he did, the first such cell in the government. Ralph de Toledano puts it this way,

> "In setting up the master cell, Ware drifted in and out of the Agriculture Department with such frequency that many people took it for granted that he was employed there. His 'cover' however, was an organization known as Farm Research, Inc." 14

Who were these "young lawyers" that were recruited and molded into the first communist cell in the American government? They were identified some fifteen years later as Lee Pressman, Nathan Witt, John Abt, Henry Collins, Charles Kramer, and Alger Hiss. All of this was going on under the nose of Mr. Tugwell.

Now the question arises, did Mr. Tugwell know what was going on, or at least did he even suspect what was going on in his department? For our answer we need to examine the events that took place on the evening of Sept. 1, 1933, in a home that was located in a Virginia suburb of Washington, D.C. The occasion was that of a dinner party at the home of Alice Barrows, an employee of the Department of Education. A special guest at that dinner was Dr. William Wirt, the superintendent of schools for Gary, Indiana, who had been the former employer of Miss Barrows and was in Washington to attend a school administrators meeting. In attendance were:

"Robert Bruere, a member of the New Deal Textile Code Advisory Board, and a World War 1 supporter of the revolutionary IWW movement; David Cushman Coyle, an employee of the Public Works Administration (PWA); Laurence Todd, a Washington representative of the Soviet news agency, TASS, and a former official of the American Civil Liberties Union; Hildegarde Kneeland, an employee of the Department of Agriculture, a member of the ACLU, and the person Dr. Wirt claimed did most of the talking about the communist plans to take over the New Deal; and Mary Taylor, also an employee of the Department of Agriculture." [15]

Dr. Wirt testified before a Congressional Investigation Committee that after the dinner an informal meeting ensued at which various members of the group began to explain what was really going on inside the New Deal Administration. Following are some excerpts from Dr. Wirt's testimony before that special committee:

" 'Brain Trusters' insist that the America of Washington, Jefferson, and Lincoln must first be destroyed so that on the ruins they will be able to construct an America after their own pattern . . I was told they believe that by thwarting our then evident economic recovery they would be able to prolong the country's destitution until they had demonstrated to the American people that the Government must operate business and commerce. By propaganda they would destroy institutions making long time capital loans — and then push Uncle Sam into making these loans. Once Uncle Sam becomes our financier he must also follow his money with control and management. . . . 'We believe we have Roosevelt in the middle of a swift stream and that the current is so strong he cannot turn back or escape from it. We believe we can keep Mr. Roosevelt there until we are ready to supplant him with a Stalin. We all think Mr. Roosevelt is only the Kerensky of the Revolution. . . . We are on the inside, we control the avenues of influence. We can make the President believe he is making the decisions for himself. . . .soon he will feel a superhuman flow of power from the flow of decisions themselves, good or bad.' . . . They were sure they could depend on the psychology of empty stomachs and they would keep them empty. The masses would soon agree that anything

should be done rather than nothing. Any escape from present miseries would be welcomed even though it should
turn out to be another misery." [16]

In the retrospective position of today we can see that
much of what had been told to Wirt came to pass as unerring-
ly as any prophecy that had ever been made, but most significant for our purposes at the moment is the fact that "Wirt
reported that the group indicated they looked for leadership
to Dr. Rexford Guy Tugwell, a radical, who was assistant to
Henry Wallace, and to Wallace himself." [17]

The important thing is, were the charges raised by Dr.
Wirt really true? Was Tugwell the inside leader to turn America into another communist state? Certainly if we examine
Tugwell's writings, statements, associations and activities up
to that point in time, it would seem to be true. It would not
seem possible that a complete communist cell could be organized and go into full activity in his department without a
man of such knowledge and experience being aware that
something was going on. The result of the investigation was
that the liberal Democrats and the liberal press set up such a
howl that the hearings were discontinued and a verdict was
never reached. However, some interesting facts have since
emerged to indicate that it was not a pipe dream that Dr.
Wirt had, but a very real experience. For example, A. A.
Berle, Jr., a New Deal official and old-time friend of Tugwell from his days at Columbia University, admitted to the
Associated Press that the conversation had taken place as Dr.
Wirt had testified, but that the government employees were
merely pulling the leg of this green out-of-town guest. This
explanation threw a lot of oil onto troubled waters, and the
incident was buried by the left-wing, hopefully forever.
However, the truth has a strange way of eventually coming
out. In an entirely different investigation some eighteen

years later the Senate Internal Security Subcommittee discovered that the same Alice Barrows, at whose home the dinner meeting was held, was a communist agent, and had been since the day she came to work for the Department of Education in 1919. In light of the admission that the conversations had actually taken place and that the hostess was a communist agent, and that the resulting events of history have demonstrated that the plan was followed almost right down to the letter, and that most of it took place under the direction of Mr. Tugwell who was an open admirer of the Soviet system, it would all appear to be just too much to be swept under the rug in the name of coincidence.

However, when the real revolution did not take place as was expected, Tugwell became disenchanted and retired from government service. In 1941 he was appointed Governor of Puerto Rico and remained at that post until 1946 when he resigned to become, at the request of Robert Hutchins, a professor of political science at the University of Chicago. He also joined Mr. Hutchins' Committee to Form a World Constitution. After two and one half years labor, the committee published to the world a document that called for complete abolition of all nations and setting up in their place nine societies. It called for complete control, planning and regulation of every phase of human life throughout the globe.

Tugwell remained at this political science post at the University of Chicago until 1957 at which time he resigned to devote more time to his writings. In 1964 he again answered the request of his long-time friend and fellow conspirator, Robert Hutchins, and joined him at The Center for the Study of Democratic Institutions in Santa Barbara, California. There Rexford Guy Tugwell answered the call to put forth a new constitution for the United States. Summing up all of his seventy-three years of socialist-communist one-world government thinking, he undertook the task. After six years of effort and some thirty-seven revisions, the editor of *The Center Magazine* states that with considerable pressure he was able to pry the document out of Tugwell's hands long enough to press it into print. It would seem that if he cannot conquer his detractors with the eloquence of his reasoning that Tugwell is determined to persist until they have all died.

CONCLUSIONS AND SUMMARY

All of the men involved with the production of the new constitution are men with long histories of socialistic associations and activities. All have either traveled in Russia personally or are fellow travelers with those that have. All have been involved one way or another with the University of Chicago and various programs to create a world government. All have either belonged to the Council on Foreign Relations personally or have been closely tied to those who were. Without a doubt, they are by their own admissions, dedicated to setting up a one-world socialist-communist government. They are not the kind of men that should be writing a constitution for the free people of America. They view the removal of our freedoms and the establishment of controls and regulations as part of interesting social experiments. It does not seem to disturb them in the least that you and I and our families are the "materials" to be used in these experiments. It does not deter them in the slightest that human lives may be hopelessly confused, disturbed and destroyed in the process of their social experiments. They apparently consider the creation of a utopian society as they view it to be of such great value that it is worth whatever price we have to pay for it. The interesting thing is that we the people have to pay the debt of their mistakes. When the social experimenter stands as the overseer and manages our lives, if he should fail, we are the ones to suffer, to bleed and die in agony while they, as though they were some sort of gods, simply recalculate their formula and begin again with some new human material.

As violently as I disagree with these men, their ideas and their methods, I do not wish to convey the thought that I believe they are motivated by a desire to see all men in the bondage of slavery. I do not believe they have such a desire. But I do believe that is the exact result of what they are trying to do. I believe that they are guilty of the very thing of which they accuse their detractors. I believe they have monumental myopia. They have become so mesmerized by their own selfish determination to rid the world of all of its evils that they can see nothing else. They love to talk of reason, and yet that is the furthest thing from their own minds. They move forward with a transfixion of purpose that rules out all reason. Their passions for triumph of good as they view it have so blinded their own vision that they cannot see the horrendous wickedness of their methods, which have caused rivers of blood to flow from their hands, having murdered millions upon millions and tortured and tormented millions more in order to bring the globe to their dream of a world socialist government. That they have chosen such a course of their own free will and choice will stand as their indictment both in this world and in the life that follows this one, just as surely as the morning sun follows the shades of night.

Chapter Three

THE CONFUSIONS

When a nation already has a constitution as the supreme law of the land and a group of individuals begin drawing up a new one, it would certainly seem to indicate some serious dissatisfaction, on their part at least, with the present one. As a prelude to an examination of their "new" ideas on the constitution, it would be helpful to understand their beliefs about the present one.

THE MYTH OF THE MYTHICAL U.S. CONSTITUTION

Mr. Tugwell states in his article entitled "Introduction to a Constitution for a United Republics of America" that several reasons existed for writing their constitution and that "the first of these was that a precious symbol had become largely a myth and myths are easily exposed."[1] To millions of Americans, including members of the legislative, judicial and executive branches of the government this just isn't so. And the fact that Mr. Tugwell states it does not make it so. It is only because of the very strong reality of the Constitution that the United States has been able to remain such a potent force in a fast-changing world. The real myth is that which is purposely being spread by the socialist-communist conspiratorial groups, that the Constitution is no longer valid. Mr. Tugwell loves to talk about the will of the people in relation to the Constitution, and yet it is not the will of the people of this nation that the Constitution should be changed; the people of America love the Constitution and all that it stands for. It is precisely because of this great love and the power that it gives the people to control their government at any time they so choose that the conspirators wish to replace it. They wish to replace it through a series of sleight of mind maneuvers that would deceive the people into thinking they were going to get a more responsive government, when in reality, they would be getting only a more domineering form of government. The statement that the Constitution is only a myth is, in reality, a confession of the kind of regard that Mr. Tugwell has always had for the Constitution. In all of his comments about the Framers of the original Constitution his intellectual contempt and total lack of understanding of the great fundamental principles upon which this government is based are clearly visible.

In examining the remarks and works of men like Tugwell we must constantly keep in mind that in spite of their great pretense to the contrary, theirs is not an unbiased, purely objective approach. It is their firm and abiding belief that the cure for all of man's ills is more and more socialism – more and more planning by them, with more and more controls and regulations upon you and me to be sure that we comply with the plans which they make to guide our lives in order to achieve the ends which they think we should achieve.

INVALID

Mr. Tugwell talks of all the things which the government has done without the Constitution's having granted the Federal government the right to do them. He cites the enormous welfare, educational, health, housing, and industrial programs with their boards and enormous regulatory powers as examples of our having dispensed with the Constitution. He cites the powers the President has successfully taken upon himself without the express authorization of the Constitution as an example of the failure of the Constitution. He sums it all up by saying, "So it was that all three branches escaped the confines of the Constitution even if liberally interpreted. The Federal government, as a whole, escaped as well from the constriction of specified powers."[2]

Indeed we will agree that all these things did indeed take place. We will readily admit that the Constitution has been violated again and again, but that does not repudiate the attacked, only the attacker. It is not the woman who has been raped that has lost her virtue, but he who has perpetrated the foul deed. So it is that we cannot detract from the power or validity of the Constitution merely on the grounds that unwise men have failed to obey the very wise guidlines which have been laid down for their benefit. This is guidelines which have been laid down for their benefit. This is tantamount to saying that the Ten Commandments are a myth and no longer valid because no one takes the trouble to observe them. Such reasoning is of satanic inspiration and would exalt the lie in the name of truth and debase the truth in the name of a lie.

IRRELEVANT

Mr. Tugwell goes on to say, "It [the Constitution] no longer described the government that really existed and no longer defined the people's relationships among each other. The Constitution, referred to so fondly by earnest patriots, no longer existed."[3]

It would seem to us that Mr. Tugwell has gotten the facts mixed up, having put the first last and the last first. It is not the Constitution which does not exist but the government which it describes. What the American people have lost is not their Constitution, but their government.

Mr. Tugwell knows and understands this as well as I do, but to reveal it would not serve his purposes. His real purpose is to convince us that we have a government but not a Constitution and that he and his fellow conspirators ought to give us a new one. Mr. Tugwell certainly should know this because, as we have already seen, he was one of the key figures in setting up the very boards, regulations, and powers which he says violate the Constitution. He is one of the fathers of our illegitimate government. Now after having committed his crime, he seeks to escape the consequences by saying that it is the Constitution that is illegitimate. I'm sure that when they raise the flag of Russian red over our sod and sing the "Internationale" he will try to tell you that it is really Old Glory and the "Star Spangled Banner." Such are the ways of those that would "give an appearance of solidity to pure wind" and turn the Constitution into a myth.

NOT REPRESENTATIVE

The next thought that Mr. Tugwell attempts to introduce into our minds is that the Constitution we now have is no longer representative of the will of the people. In reality the very thing that Mr. Tugwell and his cohorts fear most is that the Constitution **IS** the will of the people and that at any moment they may just wake up from their comfortable nap and return the government to what the Constitution says they have the right to. There is not a people on this earth, and certainly not the American people, that like a government telling them constantly what they can and cannot do. The beauty of the Constitution is that it tells us that we only have to endure so much government and no more.

But men like Tugwell and all of his associates intend to

be the government; they intend to do the telling and not to be the ones who are going to be told. You can be sure that it would greatly rankle the heart and soul of a man with the dogged determination and persistence to begin an enormous program of writing a new constitution at the age of 73 and stick with it through some 37 revisions and six arduous years all done pretty much on his own steam if he were placed under the rule of a government that told him what he could and could not do, what he must think and say and do. I can predict what a man like Tugwell would do if he had to live under the kind of government that he is trying to create for the rest of us — he would start a revolution — because he is that kind of man.

CONSISTENT CHARACTER OF MAN

Those at The Center and those of a like mind that are supporting them like to tell us that times have changed and that things are different than they were in the days when the Founding Fathers gave us the Constitution. Of course that is true, "as any fool can plainly see," to quote Li'l Abner. But even though times have changed, men and women and children have not changed, their needs have not changed. Human nature has not changed from the beginning of recorded history down to the present day.

We can read in the Old Testament of the Bible and find people struggling four and five thousand years ago with the same problems we have in our societies today. There is nothing new in free love, in lesbianism and homosexuality. God destroyed the cities of Sodom and Gomorrah because they were so steeped in these activities:

> "And they called unto Lot, and said unto him, Where are the men which came in to thee this night? Bring them out unto us, that we may know them."[4]

Used in this context the word "know" means to have sexual relations with — you will note that it was the men who wanted the use of other men. If you will read the verses that follow, you will discover that the men of that day were so perverted that even when offered Lot's two virgin daughters the men refused them.

The Apostle Paul in writing to the Romans speaks of these conditions in plain and unmistakable terms:

> "For this cause God gave them up unto vile affections: for even their women did change the natural use into that which is against nature: And likewise also the men, leaving the natural use of the woman, burned in their lust one toward another; men with men working that which is unseemly, and receiving in themselves that recompense of their error which was meet."[5]

The problems of today are no different than they were thousands of years ago. Homosexuality and lesbianism are not brought about by our modern urban living; it has nothing to do with the computer, automation or any of the other characteristics of our nonagrarian society. None of these things existed in the days of Lot or Paul, and yet they had the problem just as readily as we have it today. The problem is the product of man and not of his material environment.

The very characteristics which the over-30 generation are decrying in the youth of today are the very characteristics that were being decried in the days of Cicero and Plato. Even our hippies and yippies are not new. Ivan Turgeniev, the Russian author, describes the version he saw hanging around the Russian universities in the year 1862, over a hundred years ago:

" . . . young men and women in slovenly attire, who called in question and ridiculed the generally received convictions and respectable conventionalities of social life, and who talked of reorganizing society on strictly scientific principles. They reversed the traditional order of things even in trivial matters of external appearance, the males allowing the hair to grow long and the female adepts cutting it short, and adding sometimes the additional badge of blue spectacles."[6]

It scarcely seems possible that could be a description of young people in Russia over a hundred years ago inasmuch as it is a perfect description of a sizable group of our young people today, right down to their blue-lensed granny glasses.

Man is not one bit different today than he was when the Constitution was first drafted. His needs are no different than they were then. The only real difference is that it is now much easier to meet some of those physical needs than it was two hundred years ago. But man's hunger and need for opportunity, liberty and freedom are no less now than they were then. The beauty of the Constitution is that it was the product of wisdom distilled through the ages and condensed upon the minds of the Framers of that great document. Embedded into every line of that great work, a work whose creation was guided, in their own words, by a "finger of that Almighty hand," were the precious principles of truth, principles that are as timeless and constant as the North Star. When the astronauts blasted off into space on that historic journey to put a man upon the moon, the success of that mission was based upon principles of truth, principles that were as old as the Universe and yet as new and applicable as the future. Man and man's nature are part of that same Universe, and they are as subject to the laws which immutably guide it as any part that does or can exist. All of the learned eloquence and reason will not change the truth;

man as with God is the same yesterday, today and forever, and the Constitution of the United States offered men the greatest opportunity to go forward and unlock the Golden Promise of the Future in Freedom that had ever been given to any people.

PARADOXICAL PROBLEMS

Now we are at a time in the development of our nation where we face an enormous multitude of problems. From whence did those problems come, from the Constitution? Not hardly, since even its greatest detractors readily admit no one has been paying any real attention to it for a long time anyway. The truth of the matter is that these problems have arisen because a group of narrow-minded, tunnel-visioned individuals have taken it upon themselves to cure all of the nation's ills by ignoring that grand document and putting in its place their own questionable mentality. If ever there was going to be a witness to the validity of the Constitution and an indictment of the feeble-brained departures from it, it would be the terrible mess these very men have gotten us into. Now they want to get us out by giving us more of the same. It seems to me that it is a good deal like trying to cure diarrhea with a laxative. Seldom in the history of the world have there been men so profound at creating a problem and then pointing to the problem and declaring that it is a beautiful solution, a problem that never existed until they created it.

What was the difference between the life of an early American settler and that of a man living some five thousand years earlier? Practically none. Agriculture, trade, and industry were all on about the same plane, with some minor variations here and there. But with the advent of the great opportunities in freedom which the Constitution endowed, the world was revolutionized in far less than just two hundred years. The newest, most backward and primitive country in all the world was made to produce the greatest civilization the world has ever known, all because there was a great foundation upon which it was built, a foundation of freedom. The results of that foundation speak for themselves.

TINKERING AROUND

Then came the tinkerers – those who thought they knew best – and they began to tinker with the Constitution, ignoring it a little here and a little there, taking advantage of it wherever they could and completely by-passing it at every opportunity. Almost all of this has been done in the past forty years. And what has been the result of that past forty years? In every respect the nation has gone into a terrible decline. Unquestionably, not every problem in the nation has been directly caused by their manipulations. But, on the other hand, they have been unable to develop workable solutions to any of the problems, whether they caused them or not. That is the key point to be considered when reflecting upon their ability to produce a document that is supposed to serve as a national guide to the future. Let's take a look at the record of the tinkerers.

GROSS NATIONAL DEBT

While the Gross National Product remarkably has risen about 300% during the last twenty years, the Gross National Debt even more remarkably has risen 400% in the same period. In other words, we are going in the hole as a nation 25% faster than we are digging our way out. Today the United

States is in debt more than all of the rest of the nations of the world combined. The nation has increased its debt since the tinkerers started in 1933 by more than 18 times the entire debt from the time of George Washington in 1789 up to F.D.R. in 1933. President Nixon alone in just two years has been able to put us into debt more than all the Presidents from Washington up to Roosevelt. Our annual interest payment is now greater than our entire debt for that same period from Washington to Roosevelt. The cost of that debt is so enormous that to just pay the interest to the Federal Reserve Bank each year requires the third largest item in the nation's annual budget. That amounts to over $27,000 a minute, in interest—and that is compounded and still growing!

In 1932, the year before the tinkerers started tinkering, there were 30 million families in America and the National Budget was $4.6 billion for an average cost of $153 per family. Now that wouldn't be too bad, would it? But by 1967 the nation had grown to have 57 billion families, not quite double what it was in 1932. So what kind of increase do you think we should have in the budget — two or three times as much, or maybe even four times the budget? No. The budget for 1967 was 35 times what the budget was in 1932, even though we had less than twice as many families as there were in 1932. Now the average cost to a family is $2,980. Now you know why taxes are so high.

According to the F.B.I., crime in America is rising at a rate in excess of 10% per year. For the past two decades crime has risen over 210% while the population has only risen about 20%. This means that we are going down the road of crime ten times faster than we are growing as a nation. Every 14 minutes a woman, a girl, or a child is raped, 24 hours around the clock somewhere in the United States. Someone is murdered every 36 minutes, a burglary is committed every 16 seconds, a violent crime is committed every 48 seconds. More than half of these crimes are being committed by those under the age of 25, and a study entitled *Careers in Crime* shows that more than half of them will commit additional crimes within the next two years after their previous arrest.

IMMORALITY

Today the United States Health Department states that venereal disease is an epidemic in America, with the common cold being the only communicable disease more prevalent than gonorrhea.

We could go on and on cataloging the enormous problems that have mushroomed in this country since the tinkerers started tinkering around with the government and substituting their great "brains trust" ideas for the principles set forth so clearly in the Constitution. However, I think that you have seen enough of the evidence, and there are mountains more that go on *ad nauseum,* to see that the problems in America are not the result of our failing Constitution but rather because the men in government have failed the Constitution. This nation has always had problems and as long as there are human beings around it always will, but when a nation operates on true and correct principles the problems will increase in a closer ratio to the number of people involved. They will not skyrocket, multiplying 10 or 20 or 40 or 50 times what the population has, as we have seen within the past 40 years.

What we need is not a new constitution; what we need is to use the one we have!

SUMMARY AND CONCLUSIONS

It is not intended to blame every evil in the nation on those who have had a hand in removing our present government away from the constitutional principles and guidelines laid down by the Founding Fathers. But it is intended to show the overwhelming evidence of the fact that almost *every* aspect of American life has degenerated far more rapidly than the law of averages can account for since the tinkers began tinkering around. Some of the problem areas can easily be related to the direct action of the tinkerers, such as the skyrocketing national debt. Others, such as the problem of venereal disease, are far more indirect in their relationship. However, even though they may not be directly responsible for all the problems in America, certainly their remedies have proven to be such monumental failures over the past forty years as to completely disqualify them as architects for the future of the nation.

Chapter Four

THE COUNTERFEIT

In all of history never has there been a nation to equal the United States of America. This nation has become great because it has been founded upon a document, the Constitution, which grants to the individual unprecedented freedoms and opportunities. These freedoms and opportunities have served as the greatest motivating force that man has ever known. The Constitution has allowed men from all backgrounds the right freely to earn according to their best abilities as determined by themselves and to be able to keep what they have earned for themselves or use it as they have seen fit. However, not all men were as successful as they needed to be. There were great inequalities and suffering, even in this great land, while most of the people have enjoyed the fruits of plenty. There were prejudices and unfair restrictions placed on others which did not allow them a full opportunity to enjoy the fruits of the Constitution. To any fair-minded man, it becomes obvious that these flaws in our nation must be removed.

Many have worked long and hard to make America become what it is truly supposed to be — the land of the free, the home of the brave, with liberty and justice for all. They have worked in churches, civic organizations, scouting, Y.M. C.A., charity organizations, and a whole host of worthwhile activities to bring about great opportunities for all. But progress has not been as fast as many would like to see it; and they have decided to use other methods, such as strikes, sit-downs, and riots. Still others have sought broad legislative changes that would force people to spread the fruits of America more uniformly. Still others have worked for a new world order to solve the problems of all mankind as they think they should be solved.

Members of this last group have recently written a new constitution for America. They have written it and hope to have it adopted by exerting tremendous pressures that will force the people to accept it. They have written it as a prelude to establishing a world order. We now want to examine this document step by step.

AN IMPORTANT DIFFERENCE

While we want to examine this new constitution article by article and section by section, there is one radical departure from our present form of government which must be explained before the other interesting innovations can be fully understood and appreciated. Today we have an elected and fully representative form of government. To the vast majority of Americans it would be difficult to conceive of living under a different form of government, but that is exactly what this new constitution proposes. However, there is, at first glance, the outward appearance and form that would make it seem to be not too different. There is, for example, a President, a Senate and a House of Representatives. But there is a very far-reaching kind of difference between the Senate we have today and the one that is proposed in the new constitution.

THE NEW SENATE

The new Senate would not be elected representatives of the people as we have today but would be appointed or selected from a very small group. Their appointments to the Senate would be for life. Automatic membership in the Senate would go to former Presidents, Vice-Presidents, Principal Justices (Chief Justice), Overseers (a new government position, an appointive office to regulate elections), Chairmen of the Planning Board (a new government position, an appointive office to regulate planning), Governors General of the Republics (a new government position, an elective office similar to a State Governor) provided they have had at least seven years experience, unsuccessful Presidential and Vice-Presidential candidates who have received at least 30 per cent of the vote. Appointed by the President would be three former Chancellors (a new government position, an appointive office comparable to a Cabinet post), two officials each from civil and diplomatic service, three senior military officers. To represent the people, the President would recognize twelve non-political and nonlobbying groups or organizations he feels are representative of the national populace. Each of these groups would elect a panel of three to represent their group, and from each panel the President would pick one member to serve in the Senate. Using a similar method, the Principal Justice would select five members from the field of law, three of whom must have been former High Court members. Also, the House of Representatives would elect three of their members who have had at least six years experience to serve in the Senate.

Thus would the Senate be made up of appointed members who serve for life. They would not be elected by the people, and they could not be recalled by the people. There is no provision whatever to control or regulate this group. They would constitute one of the most powerful groups in government anywhere in the world today. They would be a law unto themselves, since, once appointed, they would answer to no one but themselves.

Now let's review the make-up of the Senate once more. They would fall into two basic groups. First, there would be those who became members of the Senate by virtue of past political experience, numbering approximately thirty members and making up about half of the Senate. Naturally some of these members would be of a like political philosophy of that of the President and because of past political associations would be inclined to favor the President's wishes for appointments by the Senate. Assuming that from forty to sixty per cent of the Senate were favorable to the President, this would give him between twelve and eighteen members he could count on for votes to sustain the appointments he desired. Now the next group would be those members directly appointed, and their number would be thirty. Of these, the President would be allowed to hand pick twenty-two members. At this point the total membership of the Senate would be no more than fifty-two members of which at the very least thirty-four, and possibly as many as forty out of the fifty-two, would be favorable to the President. This would give the President a clear majority with which to dominate the appointments of the Senate.

The next step would be the appointment by the Senate of the Principal Justice who would in turn appoint to the Senate an additional five members representing the legal and judicial fields. Inasmuch as the Senate would be controlled by the President, the Principal Justice would no doubt be someone to his liking, and the appointments made by the Principal Justice would also carry the Presidential stamp of approval. This would then give the President five more members in the Senate that would be favorable to his desires. This would give the President control over anywhere from thirty-nine to forty-five out of fifty-seven members of the Senate, again allowing him to maintain complete control.

The next step in organizing the new government would be the appointment by the Senate of an Overseer of elections, and again a Presidentially-controlled Senate could easily pick someone who would favor the political philosophy of those in power. In reality the Overseer of elections would be a political czar who would wield a power of such lasting magnitude as to make the present Chief Justice of the Supreme Court appear to be no more than president of a freshman high school class.

Although the Overseer is not to belong to any political office during his seven-year appointed term of office, there would be no way to isolate effectively his past associations and allegiances from his political past nor to separate him from his own political ideologies and the desire to make them manifest. Once a political party has qualified for recognition by the Overseer, the party must subscribe to the rules and regulations of his department if it were to be allowed to participate in the elections. In addition, he would supervise the selection of party administrators, provide the means for discussions of the issues, provide cogent information to each party and in general supervise their activities. In addition to that, the Overseer would assist the parties in nominating their candidates for the House of Representatives — the only real chance the people have of getting any voice in the government at all is through the house of Representatives, and this too is being carefully controlled so that only those favorable to those in power will run, so that heads they win and tails you lose.

No matter how it comes out when the people do not have free access to the political parties and are heavily dominated, even to the selecting of candidates by an appointed official of the then-existing government, it doesn't take someone too bright to see that this could easily turn into the most massively rigged election ever held in this country.

Still, in addition to the previous powers, the Overseer would regulate and control all nominating procedures as well as the actual campaigns and elections for the Presidential and Vice-Presidential candidates, thus assuring the powers that put him in that they would be perpetuated by a series of maneuvers that would make a great show of providing free elections in order to pacify the people; but in reality it would be a series of clever maneuvers designed to disguise the real selection of candidates, regardless of so-called party affiliation, so that no matter which one was selected it would be the power people's man. A full reading of Article II, Section 8, would be required to appreciate fully the clever intrigue and manipulations employed to create the illusion of fair and free elections.

Another interesting aspect of the Overseer and his political activities is that he also would be the paymaster to the parties. No private money is to be used; all political campaign funds would be paid out of the federal treasury from an amount accumulated for that specific purpose by a taxation of one per cent on top of each taxpayer's net taxable income. No personal or private funds could be used, except as may be authorized by the Overseer. The funds would be distributed on the basis of the number of votes in the last election. Votes then become dollars. Thus the winning party not only goes into office, but the government then awards them a nice big financial prize so that they might do even better the next time. If ever there were a scheme to get the American people to pay for the rope with which to hang themselves, this must certainly be it.

To me, the most appalling thing is the enormous audacity of the designers of this nefarious document to talk constantly of the need of representing the people, the need to give the people a voice in government, a need for the people to have a chance to speak out and be heard; and yet, if ever there were a document designed to create the illusion that the people would have a voice in the government while at the same time skinning them alive, this is it. There are those I know who will accuse me of losing my cold objectivity and moving to hot emotionalism by such comments interjected into this description of the new constitution; however, such blatant deception once discovered and exposed for what it is no longer deserves the polite respectability of objectivity. This is tyranny and oppression of the most fiendish and devilish design. It masquerades in the name of a democratic republic while in reality it is a diabolical plot to exalt raw power and to exploit the people, the wonderful people of America, the people who have given more of their blood and sweat and tears and treasure freely to all of the world than has any other people at any time. And what is to be their reward if those who have written this evil and insidious document have their way? A form of government in which they will have absolutely no say at all. A government that will control all elections, candidates and funds. A government of autocratic power that will be self-perpetuating. And the whole enormous fraud is to be paid for by the American taxpayer. In the communist nations of the world they have elections in the exact same manner; there is no difference at all. There they have only one party; here in the beginning we would be afforded the luxury of two or perhaps even three parties, but as the winner kept getting the lion's share of the purse, it would only be a short time until the Overseer would declare according to the rules of the constitution that the other parties did not represent a sufficient majority of the people to earn a place on the ballot. Then as in the communist nations of the world today, the government would have to herd the electorate to the polls on the threat that their food permit, or work permit, or housing permit would be revoked. One does not have a permit to exist in such countries unless one has some value to the powers that control the nation.

Once the Overseer had made all the necessary arrangements and the proper candidates had been selected, candidates who were, of course, friendly to the views of the President, secretly at least if not openly, the elections would be held for the House of Representatives. Since the candidates would be practically hand-picked by the President, it is easy to see that we would also have a rubber stamp House of Representatives. They in turn would elect from among their members three to serve in the Senate. Thus, it is that the government would constitutionally be turned into a dictatorship.

I am sure that there are those on the far left that will object and say that this is all hypothetical and that it might not happen that way at all. That is true. But it could happen; it could happen very easily. The key to how fast it would happen would be the Senate. Realistically speaking, it is not at all unreasonable to suppose that forty per cent of the automatic members of the Senate would be favorable to the President; and that is all that it would require for the President to gain a clear majority with which to control the entire formation of the government. Today we have a government in which such a thing cannot possibly happen because the people elect all the members of the Senate. There is no way for the President or anyone else to hand-pick the people they want. As far away as we have gotten from the government outlined by our Constitution, we the people still have control. Even though it might not actually happen the way that I have illustrated it, the fact that it easily could is too much of a risk for the people of this nation to take with the rights and freedoms of the unborn generations of Americans that are to follow. We certainly should do no less for those who follow after us than have those who have gone on before us. It is our solemn and sacred duty to pass the Torch of Freedom on to the next generation, undimmed.

Now that we understand how the Senate is to be composed and how easily it can be formed to reflect a single philosophy or owe allegiance to one or two people, we will be able to see as we go through the new constitution article by article that all of the key appointments could easily be given only to those who were part of a special power group that would perpetuate itself.

ARTICLE I — THE NEW REPUBLICS

One of the first things that one notices in the examination of this new constitution is that our country is no longer The United States of America but rather it is The United Republics of America. Gone would be familiar names like Iowa, Arkansas, California, New York, Utah, and all the rest of the fifty states; and in their place would be republics. Now perhaps some of these republics would retain the name of a dominant state that would now be incorporated within them, that is, if there were someone left with enough political pull in the new scheme of things to get the job done. Actually the new constitution doesn't deal with such trivial matters; it simply does away with the states. The republics may vary in number. According to the way that the constitution is written, there could be as few as one and as many as twenty. Twenty, however, would be the maximum number inasmuch as no republic can have less than five per cent of the total population.

ESTABLISHING THE REPUBLICS

A thirteen man or woman commission appointed by the Principal Justice (who would have been appointed by the Senate) would make a study and report its findings and recommendations to the Principal Justice. He in turn would make his report and recommendations to the Senate, who upon accepting his recommendations would establish the boundaries as he had outlined them. As far as possible, no state is to be divided, but whole states are to be incorporated within the new republics. You will note that none of the people involved in the process are elected representatives of the people: all are appointed – the commission, the Principal Justice, and the Senate – all of them are appointed. The people are to have no voice in the matter, not as to the size of the republics, their geographical configurations or their population. They are to have no say at all.

ALL POWERFUL FEDERAL GOVERNMENT

In complete contrast to the present Constitution wherein the federal government derives its just powers from the several states, under the new arrangement the republics would have whatever powers the federal government would choose to extend to them. Specifically singled out are such items as elections, subsidiary governments, taxes, public services, emergencies, police powers, treaties, currency, and trade which would be regulated by federal law and departments; and the republics could have such jurisdiction over those items to the extent that federal law granted it to them.

NO VOICE FOR THE PEOPLE

As further example of how the republics are carefully restricted and controlled by the federal government, we note that the election of the Governors General of each republic and the legislature, planning, administrative, and judicial systems would all be controlled and carefully regulated by federal restrictions. In addition to this, we discover that if, in the opinion of the national Senate, the officials of the republics were not performing satisfactorily they could be removed from office by that self-same Senate. Not only would the administrators be placed in office through the elaborate controls of the federal Overseer, but once in office they would not be answerable to the people but to the same national Senate which had appointed the Overseer to control their election in the first place.

Nowhere in the entire document is there an opportunity for the people to rid themselves of the government of a republic if they the people are dissatisfied. As long as the national Senate is satisfied, the people must endure the government of the republics. This could hardly be called government of the people, by the people, and for the people.

ARTICLE II — ELECTORAL BRANCH

The details of this article have already been given when considering the work of the Overseer. The Overseer would become the political czar of the nation. He would be in charge of and have direct authority over all elections although he might set up a very elaborate system of suboverseers in the republics and various departments of government at different levels. He would have almost unlimited power to control the electoral process of the entire nation. He would have the authority to set up regulatory boards and agencies throughout the nation. He would control the nominations of the parties, the campaigns, the elections and the funding. To wield so much power with so little in the way of checks and balances would be to make of this individual one of the most powerful men on earth with the ability to influence the future of the nation for many decades to come. There are few things which a nation of people could do that would be more foolish than to place the future of that nation so completely in the hands of so few people, especially officials who are not answerable to the people.

ARTICLE III – THE PLANNING BRANCH

This article details the formation and activities of a planning board of eleven members to be appointed by the President and presided over by a chairman. The duties and activities of the planning board would be to prepare six and twelve year plans and projected budgets for the expansion of the economy and the utilization of natural resources. The planning board would have the authority to require reports from all sectors of the public and private life in order to formulate the orderly progression of the nation's growth. While on the surface it would seem to be a good and wise thing for a nation to have long-range plans of orderly growth and development, to do so at the expense of the freedom of its people is a violation of the most fundamental rights set forth in the Declaration of Independence.

To plan and budget have been the hallmark of every truly great organization and certainly our government is no different in its need to plan and budget. But what are we to understand by such statements as, "Submissions may be required from such private individuals or associations as are affected with a public interest, including those organized as Authorities"? Or such statements as, "Developments in violation of official designation shall be at the risk of the venturer and there shall be no recourse. . ."? Taken in relation to the other articles and sections of this constitution, it can only mean one thing, and that is the submission of the private individual and his enterprise to the will of the government no matter how unrepresentative it may be of the will of the people. Not only must the individual freedom of the people be curtailed to accommodate the plans of international expansion by other nations as well: ". . . there shall be due regard to the interests of other nations and such cooperation with their intentions as may be consistent with plans for the United Republics."

The message is very clear and becomes clearer with each succeeding article and section — the people of America are to be controlled and regimented like so many animals on a farm.

ARTICLE IV — THE PRESIDENCY

There are several novel innovations in this article. One is the idea that two Vice-Presidents are better than one. On this point there may be some merit, since Congress has been somewhat concerned about Presidential successors in case of assassination and heart attacks. One of the Vice-Presidents would be in charge of Internal Affairs, handling such departments to govern the internal affairs as the President should see fit to establish. The other Vice-President would be in charge of General Affairs and would oversee such departments as finance, legal, military and foreign. Heading each of these departments would be an individual with the title of Chancellor. The Cabinet as it is known in government today would be done away with. With regard to the appointment and administration of various departments the President would have a rather free hand, much as he does today. Only when two-thirds of the Senate should object would any of the President's orders be countermanded.

There is one suggestion found in Sections 14 and 15 that may have some rather ominous results for the people. This would be the establishment of what the new constitution calls the Intendant. The duty of the Intendant would be to "supervise Offices for Intelligence and Investigation. He shall also supervise an Office of Emergency Organization . . . [and] . . . coordinate scientific and cultural studies within the government and elsewhere, and for this purpose he shall establish such agencies and organize such assistance as may be found necessary." This office would "be responsible to the President." Here, buried down at the tail end of the article is the potential to create a head of the gestapo, a secret police organization answerable only to the President, a President who has the potential ability to select his own Senate and thus to control all appointments by them, a President who through his Overseer can control all of the election of the nation; and then add to this the power to create his own secret police organization and you have given him all of the necessary requirements to become the dictator. Then you add to this the fact that according to section one he would be elected for a nine-year term, giving him all the time that he would need to consolidate his power to the extent that he would no doubt stay in office as long as he so desired or until forces in the Senate politburo were sufficiently organized to overthrow him.

I fear that should a constitution such as this one ever be adopted we would see a never-ending struggle for more and more power by men who thought they could gain it and more and more bloodshed as they sought to accomplish it.

We would see a series of Stalins, Krushchevs, and Kosygins. Meanwhile, as elsewhere in the world where such enormous power is contained in the hands of so few, the American people would have less and less.

ARTICLE V — LEGISLATIVE BRANCH

This article is divided into two divisions — Division A, having to do with the Senate, and Division B, having to do with the House of Representatives.

We have already examined the method of forming the Senate and its make-up and have seen that it is a very powerful branch of the government that is not answerable to the people. We have also seen that it could easily have the polarity of its political nature controlled by the President. Since the Senate members are appointed for life and are in reality the most powerful group within the government, having the responsibility of making most of the key appointments, it is extremely dangerous that there is no way for the people of the nation to control them. There is no provision to remove them from office should the people be dissatisfied and feel that they were not reflecting the will of the nation.

While the Senate has the privilege of recommending legislation, it does not, under this arrangement, have the power to create it. This function is reserved to the House of Representatives. However, the Senate has the power to veto all laws passed by the House unless the House shall override the Senate veto by a two-thirds vote. The object of this method of lawmaking is to reflect more clearly the will of the people in the laws of the land and to speed up the process of making laws. While the object is a laudable one, there is some serious doubt as to the wisdom of such a procedure as has been outlined. It is very doubtful, because of the Senate-dominated department of the Overseer of elections, that any Representatives would be allowed to be elected who would really represent the people in the first place. In the second place, there is considerable evidence to indicate that the worst laws to ever be enacted were those that have been successfully railroaded through Congress. Therefore it is doubtful that speeding up the enactment of law would be of any great benefit to the nation.

Before leaving our consideration of the Senate, we should examine another of the unique names given to a new government post—that of the Watchkeeper. He would be appointed by the Senate to act as a watchdog over all of the many agencies and departments of the government and would report to the Senate any observance of wrongdoing or inefficiency. He would also recommend new services or the removal of old ones. Naturally he would need a large department of federal employees to check up on all of the other large departments of federal employees, costing you the taxpayer another quarter of one per cent tacked on to your net taxable income.

The Founding Fathers were aware that the combination of both ambition in some and negligence on the part of others could create unresponsive government that could both infringe upon your rights and also fail to serve you. They were aware of the need to protect you from such an eventuality. They were also aware of the dangers of watchdog agencies that can become too ravenous and powerful. Therefore they devised a system of government that relied upon the natural counterambitions of three departments completely separate and autonomous from the others. Thus they created the executive, the legislative, and the judicial branches so that these departments might serve as counterbalances to each other, thus reducing greatly both the cost and the dangers; and of course it has worked remarkably well. Once we begin to remove this triangular check-and-balance system, we have to create special institutions to do what was once a natural by-product of that system of government.

THE HOUSE OF REPRESENTATIVES

There are quite a number of sections under this division of Article V which have to do with the areas of technical operations of the House and which detail routine procedures and responsibilities for lawmaking. We shall not take the time to consider these, but there are several sections of special interest that have to do with items concerning the freedom and welfare of all the people of the nation.

Section 4 details instructions that "no quotas, and no nations favored by special rates, unless by special acts requiring two-thirds majority" shall interfere with or regulate free trade with all nations of the world. Thus the nation would not consider the welfare of any of its own industries more than it would the welfare of any industry of any nation in the world, and no distinction would be made as to the political or economic philosophy of the nations involved. Under the provisions of this section, American labor would have to compete in the marketplace with the products of slave labor in communist countries. Obviously, if our economy were suddenly thrown wide open to the products of slave labor, the value of American labor would be sharply diluted and the income of the average American family would drastically decline. Meanwhile, the effect on raising the standard of living of the enslaved people of the world would be minimal to say the least.

Section 5 provides for the establishment of national banks for the purpose of controlling credit and as a depository of the savings of the people. They would also manipulate the medium of exchange and provide for the control of coinage of money. Some private banks would be allowed, but they would be controlled by the government.

This section would result in the citizen's losing the right to invest his earnings at a financial institution where he might be able to earn a higher interest rate, as the government would set a standard rate for all institutions. In addition to this, government control of all savings and depository institutions would cause the depositor's savings to be in constant jeopardy, subject to seizure and confiscation by the government at any unannounced moment. It would result in a monopoly that could result in deteriorated service. Credit would be extended more on the basis of political connections than on business qualifications. The financial institutions would simply become a tool of the government to manipulate the economy of the people for the welfare of the government.

Section 6 provides for the establishment of national insurance companies to provide for protection of risk from loss due to unforeseeable tragedies. The participation in these insurance programs on one's life, health and property would no doubt be made compulsory, as with Social Security today, and the money would be forcibly removed from your pay. Also, as with Social Security, it would no doubt cost you considerably more than you could conceivably hope to get back from it. This section makes me think of the Mafia's protection racket; you pay up or else.

Section 7 provides for the nationalization of the "facilities for communication, transportation, and others commonly used and necessary for public convenience." Once the communication media have been nationalized "for the public's protection," of course, those in power would have at their disposal the most gigantic propaganda machine ever created. The people of the nation would know only what those in power wanted them to know. The Founding Fathers recognized the need for freedom in the area of communication and so guaranteed freedom of the press in the original constitution in the Bill of Rights, that no group of evil and conspiring men could have at their disposal such a giant tool with which to deceive the public. Even today with the great deal of freedom that exists the public has a lot of trouble in getting the truth because of the obvious focusing of the news media on issues favorable to certain groups and parties within our society. One can readily imagine if the media were all nationalized what little chance we the people would have of knowing the truth.

Sections 8, 9 and 10 spell out the real purpose of this entire document — that is, "to assist in the maintenance of world order" and "to vest such jurisdiction in international legislative, judicial, or administrative organizations as shall be consistent with the national interest."

Nowhere is it spelled out what is "consistent with the national interest." Is it the pouring of billions of dollars of the average American's money into communist nations? To Paul Hoffman, the man who was Chairman of the Board of the organization that produced this document, it is. We know that because he has personally supervised, as we have already pointed out, the distribution of millions upon millions of dollars of American taxpayer's money to communist nations. Does it mean the yielding up to an international world court our rights of sovereignty, and the obedience to laws and regulations of an international world organization, and the taxation of Americans to pay for the development of the rest of the world? Is that what it means? Yes, that is exactly what it means because it is so spelled out in section 10 as follows: "To assist other people who have not attained satisfactory levels of well-being; to delegate the administration of funds, whenever possible, to international agencies; and to invest in or contribute to the furthering of development in other parts of the world."

The American taxpayer would be worked, starved, and bled to death in order to redistribute the wealth of the world according to an old Marxian concept — from each according to his ability to each according to his need. Obviously, since we have such great ability and the others have such great needs, we would be the givers and they would be the receivers. While it is surely much more blessed to give than it is to receive, it is not more blessed to have it taken. It is morally wrong to take from the producer and allow an international agency which has had no part in the production to be charged with its distribution.

Under this constitution the people of the nation would have great difficulty obtaining any representation even in their own government, and they would have absolutely no representatives in an international agency. Even today in the so-called United Nations, the people of America have no representation; there are some representatives of the nation there but they were appointed and do not truly represent the people. Yet the people of the nation are heavily taxed to pay for the United Nations and the work of its many agencies. This is taxation without representation in its worst form. It was over this very principle that our forefathers fought to create this nation, and the ratios weren't nearly as bad as they are now.

The people of America have never wanted or tried to shirk their fair responsibility to the peoples of the world. The objection to this section is not intended to convey the thought that we ought to crawl off in our own little corner and let the rest of the world go by. But the American people should be allowed to give to the poor, the underprivileged and the downtrodden according to the dictates of their own conscience, and funds should not be conscripted from them without their consent. Also, the distribution of those funds should not be placed in the hands of some third party who has no real interest in the sweat and toil that was required to produce those funds that he so generously has received. The concept of taking from those that have earned, those that have produced, and giving it to those who have not, is a concept of leveling down of the people of the world rather than one of building up the people of the world.

Section 17 would provide for the establishment of a Board of Arbitration which would provide "conclusive arbitration." Conclusive arbitration means that whatever the Board says labor is going to get, labor is going to get, and whatever it says management is going to pay, management is going to pay. In this situation both labor and management would lose. There is no freedom in "conclusive arbitration."

Section 19 is "to enact such measures as will assist families in making adjustments to future resources, using estimates concerning population which have been made by the planning board." This means that families would be told where they could live and work according to how they fit into the overall plans for the development of the state and its resources.

They would also be told if they could have children and, if so, how many. This, of course, is already being seriously advocated by many of the liberal thinkers of the day. If you were not one of the chosen ones to have children, the government could have the right to have you sterilized so that you could not reproduce. Those with unauthorized pregnancies would have compulsory abortions performed to terminate them. It is even possible this could be extended to the point that upon testing of the population those not deemed useful to society would be put to sleep.

Once again we see that the society of the state would be supreme and the freedom of the individual would be as nothing. The individual would exist for the state, rather than the state existing for the individual.

These are some of the more pertinent instructions on laws to be enacted by the members of the House of Representatives. The question now is, whom do they represent?

ARTICLE VI — REGULATORY BRANCH

This article provides for the office of the Regulator and a National Regulatory Board to serve under his direction. It would be the duty of the Regulator and the many commissions and agencies which he might form to help him to regulate the affairs of all business enterprises. As will be seen from an examination of the following sections of this article, nothing in the field of business is to be left to the individual citizen. All business will be closely regulated by the government. Without government approval no business enterprise would even be allowed to exist. The scope of the business' activities would be given to it — its methods of operation, the number of employees, and the resulting amount of profit allowed would all be detailed to the business by the government. Violators would be heavily fined and/or imprisoned. Under this constitution it will be seen again and again that the citizens of the nation shall be the last to be considered and that the government shall be the first.

Section 2 grants the Regulator the authority to "Charter all corporations or other enterprises."

Section 3 grants that the chartered enterprises are to form self-regulating authorities over their industry or trade in order to regulate its practices. Those not complying with the resulting codes established would have their charters revoked.

The Authorities would have a five-man governing board, three of which would be appointed by the Regulator to represent the public; and they would be compensated for their services by the membership of the Authorities. The Regulator would also under authority of this section "approve or prescribe the distribution of profits to stockholders, allowable amounts of working capital, reserves and costs, and all other practices affecting the public interest."

Section 5 provides for the regulation of mergers and acquisitions.

Section 6 provides for the regulation of prices and for ecological considerations.

Section 8 provides the authority to establish tax-free, non-profit foundations and organizations. For the favored few?

Section 9 provides for the authority to regulate marketplaces and storehouses.

Section 10 provides the authority for the Regulator to declare which enterprises must operate in the public interest and the rules and regulations whereby they must operate.

Section 11 provides for the establishment of commissions to regulate government-operated enterprises. These may or may not operate at a profit. If previous experience is any indication, they will most assuredly operate at a loss.

ARTICLE VII — JUDICIAL BRANCH

This article provides for the restructuring of the judicial system of the nation. It would consist at the top of the Principal Justice who would be appointed by the Senate for a twelve-year term, but could be subject to recall after six years of service.

Section 2 grants the authority to the Principal Justice to become the czar of the judicial system of the nation. He would really answer to no one but himself and would have absolute and complete authority over the entire judicial system. He would appoint all members of the courts throughout the land and, with the assistance of those he chose to make up a Judicial Council, he would make the rules of the courts. Once again we see this terrible weakness of placing enormous far-reaching and autocratic power into the hands of a man who has no checks and balances to protect the people from his becoming a ruthless tyrant. Under such a system, the idea of a fair trial could easily become a mere facade, a mockery of justice.

Section 3 provides for the formation of a Judicial Assembly to be convened annually or at the discretion of the Principal Justice to consider whatever matters he might choose to bring before it. This Assembly is to be made up of representatives of all levels of the judicial system and they would select three candidates from which the Senate would pick the succeeding Principal Justice. The Principal Justice would be the one to select the Assembly, to call its meetings and to define its agenda. What we would have here is the thinking of one man reflected again and again, as he would almost instinctively choose only those who thought as he thought to serve in the Assembly. Assuredly it would not have to be that he would select only men like himself, but he could; and it is these unjust eventualities that a just constitution must guard against.

Section 4 provides for the formation of a Judicial Council of five members to be selected by the Principal Justice to serve with him in making up the rules of the courts, codes of ethics and recommendations when necessary for constitutional revisions or amendments.

As in the previous section, we see once again the tendency to place all power into the hands of the Principal Justice.

In the eventuality that his judgments were not inclined toward justice for all, it would be reflected in his appointments to the Judicial Council and in the rules and regulations of the courts. It is not right and it is not just that one man should have such far-reaching influence over the operation of the courts. The fact that the Supreme Court has reversed itself in recent years is evidence that even a panel of men selected by various men and of differing backgrounds, may not reach a decision that another panel of equally concerned men would consider in harmony with the law. If it is true that such a panel of men might not see the law perfectly, it is even more evident that a panel selected by a single man could be in grave error.

Section 7 provides the courts with the authority to determine whether a person accused of a criminal act shall have a trial by jury or by a tribunal of three judges and whether the trial shall be investigatory or adversary. This is the system that is used in communist nations of the world, and of course they are famous for their "fair trials."

It is also the same system that was used in ancient Europe and England. It was mainly over this sytem of prerogative courts, the right to determine the kind of trial and the elimination of so-called investigatory trials that the 2,000 English barons forced the King of England to grant the Magna Carta. To reinstate the system of prerogative courts is to step back into the 13th Century and to reduce the average man to nothing more than a pawn before the court.

First the accused would be submitted to an investigatory proceeding, more commonly known as interrogation. Once sufficient information had been extracted the victim would be submitted to a court of three judges and he would be found guilty. In those cases where the publicity would serve the purposes of the state, a jury that already knew how to vote could be selected and the victim could be put on display for the edification of anyone else who might get the notion he wanted to try the same thing. To leave it up to the court to decide what the accused would receive by way of a trial is to remove the barest essentials of any hope of a fair trial.

This section concludes with the magnanimous declaration that "the court shall consider his [the accused] belief that the statute was invalid or unjust."

With the first reading of this quote, one might naturally think that the court will actually consider the law which the accused claims to be unjust, but the key phrase here is "consider his belief." Therefore the court would instead take the attitude of not that the law was not applicable, or that it is unjust, or that the accused might even be innocent of any violation at all; no, it is going to "consider his belief" that the law was not applicable to his actions. What is on trial is the belief of the individual. The court is generously going to think about, ponder over, the belief of the accused that he did not violate the law. It is not a question under this wording as to whether the individual is innocent; it is merely an examination as to whether his intentions were good or bad. The attorneys in Russia who have been assigned as counsel for the defense of those Americans accused of violating the law have always been advised not to plead innocent and contest with the court, but to do everything within their power to show a repentant and servile attitude so that the intent of the actions of the accused would show in the best possible light. It is not a question of guilt or innocence; it is a question of intent. When the state is all-powerful and you go before the state court, you are already determined to be guilty or you would not be there; the question to be resolved is your intent with regard to the law.

What a far cry this is from the rights guaranteed under the present Constitution, wherein an individual is innocent until he is proven guilty by an openly selected jury. This new constitution is offered to us as a supposed improvement over the system that we now have; but if it, or anything even close to it is ever enacted in this nation, it would mean the end of justice and the exaltation of tyranny.

Section 9 grants to the Principal Justice along with his Judicial Council or the President the right to grant pardons for crimes against the state.

Section 12 makes it mandatory for all other branches of the government to accept and enforce judicial decrees. This would have the effect of making the Principal Justice a dictator, inasmuch as the courts would rule upon the constitutionality of various laws and acts of both public and private activities.

Section 14 grants the High Court of the Constitution the power to decide the constitutionality of law, actions, litigations, powers, interpretations, and international and United Nations agreements. It is obviously intended that there are to be numerous incidents where citizens of the nation are to be delivered up to the United Nations World Court for violations considered to be out of harmony with treaties and agreements made in connection to our responsibility to feed, clothe, and develop the nations of the world as outlined in Article V, Division B, Section 10 of this new constitution.

It is most interesting to note the great emphasis on the court's power and need to determine the constitutionality of so many measures when that is the precise reason cited as justification for a new constitution in the first place. Mr. Tugwell is fond of mentioning again and again the fact that the courts are now determining what is constitutional so often that we need a new constitution to spell out more clearly what is constitutional and what is not. Yet in his own constitution he is so unsure of what is constitutional and what is not that he has found it necessary to set up a special court to determine just this. There seems to be no limit to his ability to turn the facts around to suit his own purposes.

ARTICLE VIII – GENERAL PROVISIONS

This article sets forth the rights and privileges of the various citizens of the nation as they are generally set forth in the present Constitution with three notable exceptions.

Section 1 authorizes the formation of a Citizenship and Qualifications Commission which would consist of thirteen members appointed by the President and a group of appointed officials which he controls. "Qualifications for participation in democratic procedures as a citizen of the United Republics and eligibility for national offices shall be subject to repeated study and to redefinition by law"; it shall be the responsibility of this commission to execute this directive. This is a thinly veiled maneuver to refine the rights of citizenship insofar as having the right to vote and work in the service of the government is concerned to a select few that will cooperate with the powers of government.

Section 3 guarantees the right of citizens to practice religion, but it also prohibits the government from encouraging religion. This would of course mean the removal of the name of God from all coins and currency, from any official government document, or publication, building, or utterance. It would do away with prayer as part of government meetings or ceremonies. It would eliminate the use of the Bible in swearing-in ceremonies. It would do away with the Chaplains in the House and Senate, as well as the military services. It would remove God from the national life of the country and cause this nation to be dependent upon its own frail resources.

In his famous Farewell Address to the Congress, George Washington declared, "Of all the dispositions and habits which lead to political prosperity, religion and morality are indispensible supports. ... Reason and experience both forbid us to expect that national morality can prevail in exclusion of religious principle." This nation was founded and made great upon the basis of a national committment to God; to turn away from Him at the hour of our greatest need is to commit national suicide. Abraham Lincoln knew and understood this. He solemnly declared, "God rules this world — it is the duty of nations as well as men to own their dependence upon the overruling power of God, to confess their sins and transgressions in humble sorrow . . . and to recognize the sublime truth that those nations only are blessed whose God is the Lord."

Section 12 bars all citizens from having the right to bear or even possess any lethal weapons. Once disarmed, citizens would be left defenseless against any power that should decide to oppress or abuse them. The Founding Fathers of this nation had seen what the oppressive governments of England and Europe had done to the defenseless people of those lands and vowed that such would not be the case in this nation. This is one of those fundamental rights to which every individual is endowed by his Creator, the right to defend himself.

The excuse for usurping his right is, of course, that accidents and crimes are the result of weapons. But this is not true; crime is the result of poor morality. Those with moral attitudes which allow them to engage in criminal behavior will use that criminal behavior to secure for themselves those weapons that are necessary for the pursuit of their crimes.

Laws of prohibition did not eliminate alcohol from society, nor marijuana, L.S.D. or other drugs. Such laws will also fail to eliminate guns and other weapons from the criminal element of our society. Then only the honest citizen will be left defenseless. While it may be true that the elimination of weapons from the average home would reduce the number of accidents, it may also be equally true that the increase in deaths and injuries that would result from the lawless element knowing that the average home and business were defenseless, and therefore easy victims, would more than offset any gains to be made through the prevention of a few accidents.

For the benefit of those humane-minded citizens interested in the preservation of life and limb, it might be well to note that according to the National Safety Council, there were more than 22,000 people in 1970 who lost their lives due to auto accidents involving drunken driving.[1] So it might be well in the interest of the fact that at least ten times as many people are killed each year due to the misuse of alcohol as firearms to begin by ridding society of alcoholic beverages. Or perhaps since there were some 17,500 people who died due to falls, we should outlaw all ladders in the interest of safety, or perhaps it would also be well to outlaw all swimming because there were some 7,300 drownings in 1970. Of the top ten causes of accidental deaths, the use of firearms with 2,300 ranks seventh. It would seem much wiser to start a little closer to the top of the list where so much more needs to be done rather than to begin by outlawing guns and leaving the honest populace defenseless in the face of armed attack by the ordinary criminal or the organized efforts of such groups as the "Panthers" or "Weathermen" when the ordinary police force would not be adequate for the defense of the populace.

The first step will, no doubt, be the registration of the ownership of all firearms. Then in a short time the owners will find that their weapons are confiscated by the government on some trumped-up safety law that had been passed quietly. That is the way it happened in Czechoslovakia in 1949; now they live behind the Iron Curtain of Communism, without any choice.[2] We in America must never let this happen to us; we must always insist on the fundamental right of self-defense, the right to own and bear arms when it is necessary. This right must not be abridged; it must not be infringed upon.

ARTICLE IX – GOVERNMENTAL ARRANGEMENTS

This article has nine sections and deals with the rules and regulations concerning the establishment of various assistants in different departments of government. It describes payment and protection procedures for various members of government service. It also outlines impeachment proceedings by the Senate and the Judicial Council.

ARTICLE X – AMENDMENT

This article has two sections both of which deal with the amendment procedures. The only point of significance is that when an amendment, or for that matter any other item of business, is brought to the people for a vote, it would be considered accepted unless a majority of the people vote *against* it.

ARTICLE XI – TRANSITION

This article details the authority, procedures, rules and regulations to govern the transition from one form of government to the other.

Section 1 grants the President the authority to "assume" the powers, appointments, and spend the funds he deems necessary in order to implement the new constitution. To grant someone the authority to "assume" powers to set up a new government is granting him the authority to become a dictator. Under such an arrangement there would be no checks and balances to restrain the President from making the new government his government. There are no restrictions placed upon the President as to the amount of time that he may "assume" the authority to implement this new form of government. Thus, once he had assumed the dictatorial powers necessary to set up the government he might simply keep them and never quite get around to forming a constitutional government as it had been outlined. Once again we see that there are no checks and balances to control the President.

Section 2 states that the Senate would be considered a working body when it had reached half its strength, for the purpose of making appointments to government offices and implementing the new constitution. This would mean that a clever and fast-working President could quickly appoint his 22 members to the Senate, declare them a quorum for the purpose of making appointments, and have them appoint whomever he should dictate. Thus could the President almost overnight create a dictatorship of immense proportions.

Section 3 simply states that until the new has taken over the old shall continue to function.

Section 4 states that all previous methods of government shall cease to function when replaced by the new form of government and that the President should appoint a commission to advise him as to what laws and procedures he should declare unconstitutional.

Section 5 outlines the previously discussed thirteen-man commission appointed by the Principal Justice to set up the boundaries and to outline the formation of the republics.

Section 6 designates that the constitutions of the individual republics shall be created by a committee composed of members of the highest courts within the states that are to be incorporated into the republic. A special convention of 100 delegates would be selected by the elections Overseer in a special election. If these members of the convention reject the constitution presented to them, it would be revised accordingly and resubmitted; and if it again be rejected, it would be revised again and considered valid. In spite of all the talk about rights and democracy being the need for this new constitution, I find very precious little of it here. How can a convention of only one hundred, selected in a special, controlled election by citizens who would have to meet special requirements in order to have the right and privilege of voting be able to select a truly representative group of only one hundred to represent all of the people of the republic? Do not forget that Robert Hutchins, Chairman of the organization that produced this document and of whom Mr. Tugwell said that his view "would probably come closest to being the kind of thing we wanted," is on record as being against the universal right to vote. It would seem to me that this document has been deliberately written to create the impression of giving the people a voice in the government while through a clever series of maneuverings it would actually be excluding their voice. Not only would constitutions be voted on by a very narrow and non-representative group of people, if they should reject the document twice, it would have some modifications made; and then they would have to live with it, like it or not.

Section 7 provides the President with the power to appoint Governors Generals of the various republics until such time as elections could be held. Regular state governors and officers would continue to function until their work had been taken over by the government of the republic.

Sections 8, 9 and 10 simply outline the need for haste in implementing the new constitution and the authority to delete certain sections of the article on transition as they are completed.

CONCLUSION AND SUMMARY

This new document offered in the name of democratic republics to preserve and protect the rights of the people is a counterfeit. It has the language and form of a valid constitution, but it is a fraud. It does not deliver what it is supposed to deliver; and that is what constitutes a deception, a deception of the greatest magnitude and bitterest of disappointments. The people of this nation could be fooled, could be duped into believing that this document would hold out the solution to our troubled times. Then after they had voted it in, they would wake up too late, wake up to realize that chains had been forged around their legs. They would come to realize that the President is now a dictator, that the Senate is nothing more than a socialist Politburo. From morning till night through all the government-controlled media they would be fed nothing but propaganda. Their children would be brainwashed at school to believe in the new line and that what is good is what advances the cause of the state, and that includes denying God and telling on your parents. God would be denounced as a backward nonscientific superstition. Industries would be commanded and controlled by the government and no man would be able to buy or sell without the approval of the state. Properties would be confiscated by the government for redistribution, but the only redistribution would be to the state. Fine homes, resorts, stores and office buildings would be possessed for the use of the workers of the rapidly growing government with all of its great multitude of police state boards, checking, controlling, spying and reporting on every phase of life. Power-hungry administrators willing to bend the truth for the furtherance of their own careers would not be above enlarging upon minor violations or even fabricating them about some poor unfortunate. The right to citizenship and the privilege of voting would be narrowed down to only those few who would vote the right way. The wages would drop because of open competition with slave labor from around the world; taxes would soar to pay for the new world order that the new government would be part of. There would be weeping and wailing and gnashing of teeth as the people realized that they had sold their birthright for a mess of pottage.

Chapter Five

THE CATASTROPHE

REGULATORY BOARDS

If we will just open our eyes and examine the things that are going on all around us in the affairs of state, we will see that we are already being conditioned and prepared for the acceptance of the ideas expressed in the new constitution. We now have the regulatory boards to regulate prices, and even more significantly we learn that these boards are concerned that the corporations and businesses which they regulate must not make excessive profits. Who is to decide what is excessive profits? Why, the members of the regulatory boards, of course. Labor is not going along with these boards, charging that they favor big business. The conspirators do not really intend for these boards to work, because they are only on a temporary footing. They want someone to rebel enough to have an excuse to get in a permanent setup under a new constitution. But we are being conditioned. We are getting used to the idea that we no longer have free enterprise; we are getting used to regulatory boards that control wages and prices and profits. Soon we will be so used to it we will think nothing of it when the new constitution is proposed.

Carefully they have hammered away at one central theme—the cumbersome way in which the Congress of this nation acts as a millstone around the neck of the President. They do not want a president; they want a dictator—that is what the new constitution gives us—and they are preparing us for the reception of that idea under the guise that our present method of government doesn't give the President enough latitude to move in case of emergencies. They soon intend to prove this to us by creating an emergency and then deliberately causing the key men in Congress to hamper the President, in order to make the point perfectly clear.

SPEAKING OUT

Leading out in the attack on the Constitution was Senator J. William Fulbright in a speech before the faculty and students of Stanford University in 1961. Said Mr. Fulbright: "The President is hobbled in his task of leading the American people to consensus and concerted action by the restrictions of power imposed on him by a constitutional system designed for an 18th century agrarian society far removed from the centers of world power." Mr. Fulbright went on to say many other unkind things about the Constitution, but that will suffice to show his position.

President John F. Kennedy stated on August 28, 1962, perhaps because a speech writer slipped it in there: "... the Constitution was written for an entirely different period in our nation's history." And he stated that it was not an "automatic light to the future." Placed in the context of the speech those remarks created the concept in the mind of the listener that there might be something better to guide us into the future than the Constitution.

In his column of December 10, 1963, Walter Lippmann stated that the legislative programs of the President were not able to become enacted with sufficient speed because of the cumbersome working of the Congress and suggested that another method of government might be more suitable, stating: "Whether the solution is authoritarian, as under Salazar, Franco, and deGaulle, or whether it is a coalition which suspends party conflicts, the common element is the liberation of the executive from the paralyzing grip of the representative assembly." Mr. Lippmann was willing to accept a dictatorship or a single-party government as a viable solution. The Founding Fathers knew that hasty and ambitious men would want to run the government in just those ways and deliberately created a form of government that ground slowly in order to be the more sure that it ground fairly and finely. If it had not been for that Divinely inspired Constitution with its checks and balances, our government would have long ago fallen to the many individuals and groups that have sought to take it over.

McGeorge Bundy, presidential advisor to Presidents Kennedy and Johnson, and president of the Ford Foundation, stated in a speech in March of 1968, as reported by the Associated Press, the following remark: "The powers of Congress continue to predominate over those of the President except in the most unusual moments . . . The simplest demonstration of the weakness of the Executive Branch is its subordination to the Congress in matters of appropriation and taxation." As with Lippmann, Bundy is anxious to change our form of government into a dictatorship so that the President can move with a free and unrestrained hand.

It is interesting to note that all of the gentlemen quoted who have attacked the validity of the Constitution in our times are members of the private Foreign Relations Club that was founded and is still directed and funded by the Super-Rich of the nation; it is the Council on Foreign Relations. The Council or CFR, as it is commonly known, has outlined for the past thirty years a series of goals and objectives for the United States government. By what is not a strange coincidence, all of these goals coincide with the goals of the American Communist Party.

It has become a popular intellectual pastime in recent

months on college campuses and in private organizations to debate the pros and cons of the viability of the Constitution in our modern society. We are being prepared to think about alternatives. You can be sure that the tempo will soon increase in these conditioning exercises. Such popular figures as Eugene McCarthy have entered into these debates.

CONTROLLED POLITICS

We also see proposals for government-sponsored, paid for and controlled political campaigns. The bills have already been through Congress and received a great deal of play in the media. This is just to prepare us so that the idea of government-controlled elections will not seem strange when we get the new constitution. This is the way they regulate the elections in Russia and China and Cuba, and you know how fair they are.

PLANNING COMMISSIONS

Now we are seeing the President appoint commissions, with the glorified title of Presidential Commission on Planning. They study what they believe to be trends and future needs of the nation and are making recommendations to him for future legislation, to be recommended by him. We are being conditioned to accept the idea of the planning boards that are outlined in the new constitution. Our lives will be outlined, pre-planned from the cradle to the grave.

NATIONAL POLICE FORCE—THE POLICE STATE

We are seeing the present riots, crime, and civil disorders, which have been largely sponsored by the Super-Rich, used as the excuse for more and more Federal assistance to the local police. We are seeing the recommendations that more and more of our police should attend a National Police Academy.

Next we will see Federal advisors to the police in the various localities that are now accepting the Federal handouts in order to upgrade their police departments. We are being conditioned to accept the idea of a national police force—a gestapo—as is proposed in the new constitution. By the time that the new constitution is seriously proposed in public debate, none of the ideas will be new.

CONTROLLED EDUCATION

More and more we are hearing about and seeing Federal aid to education becoming a reality and a common everyday occurrence. Of course with the aid come certain restrictions and regulations that must be complied with. Soon the process of education will be state controlled from the Federal level. Our children will be taught what the government wants them to be taught, not what you and I as parents want our children to be taught. We are being conditioned to relinquish our rights and control over the schools by their bribing us to give up the responsibility to fund them. We are being conditioned to accept the concept of big brother government operating the schools just as it is outlined in the new constitution.

NOTHING NEW

What we are seeing today and will continue to see even more of in the coming weeks and months is the introduction to the American people of every major concept that is embodied in the new constitution. The people of this nation will be so used to the ideas contained therein that these ideas will not seem the least bit strange or foreign to the traditions of American life. Nothing will be new; but it will all be so helter-skelter, so temporary, all that will remain is to consolidate and finalize them into the new constitution. And of course we will be brainwashed with the idea that there is no better way that we could honor the great American Patriots that founded this nation than, on the eve of the two hundredth anniversary, to adopt a new constitution in the same revolutionary spirit possessed by our Founding Fathers of going forward, unchained from the past.

ATTACKING THE U.S. CONSTITUTION

Those who have been working with the Super-Rich for many years have begun a slow but steady and insidious attack on the present Constitution. They have not attempted at this point to dissuade the public in general of their love of the Constitution. They have contented themselves with working over the thinking of the opinion molders in our society. They have made speeches and written articles to be received by the top socialist scholars of the nation, educators, news media personnel, ministers, lawyers and businessmen.

STATE RESOLUTIONS

In the March 1971 issue of the police magazine, *Law & Order*, editorial writer W. Cleon Skousen, a nationally recognized authority on the conspiracy, reports on page 77 that while most of us have been busy with other things, the Super-Rich have mobilized their forces and quietly gone from one state legislature to the next. Thus far they have been able to induce a total of 33 state legislatures to pass a resolution calling for a new Federal constitutional convention. All they need for the required majority to bring this to pass is 34 states. Just one more is all that it will take. Obviously, it will not be long before they obtain one more. Then all will be in readiness for that propitious moment. They have the working model completed; they have the radicals primed to create riots; they have the economy in the palm of their hand and ready to fall into an economic crisis; they have leading and prominent individuals ready to speak out for the new constitution, and they have the call from the states for the constitutional convention.

HOW CLOSE ARE WE?

As I write these lines in the spring of 1972, I feel that we are within a few months of seeing a gigantic, a monstrous, all-out campaign to install a new constitution. It may begin with the disturbances that will arise out of the '72 elections. It may be that all current political structures will be made to look so bad that only the emergence of a fresh new party, one that has all the support and financing of the Super-Rich, such as the Common Cause Party, will be brought forward. Riding on his white horse as the knight in shining armor will be someone like Ralph Nader, clean and neat, unassociated with the dirty mess of politics, who will come forward to say that we need a new constitution so that such terrible things as have happened with all these dirty secret deals and under-the-table agreements that have been revealed recently can never happen again. In the midst of the clamor and confusion, in the midst of economic chaos and civil turmoil, in the midst of discredited politicians, it will all seem so logical and so plausible. Golden promises of guaranteed annual income, housing, food, medicine, old-age care, child care, education, and on and on will the honeyed words drip from the lips of the man (whoever he will be) who will appear to be so pure, so wholesome, so unassociated with the dirty world of politics; and so desperate will the people of the nation be in the midst of the worst depression the nation has ever seen that it will all look like manna from heaven. Like Esau on his knees, starving and begging for food, will we the people of the nation come to our leaders, and they like Jacob will say, "Give us your birthright"—our Inspired

Constitution"— and in exchange for a few little regulations we shall impose upon you, we will save you; you will never have to want again. Thus shall the American people be induced to sell their birthright of freedom for a mess of potage! How close is it? It is as close as tomorrow!

WHAT CAN BE DONE?

Most Americans want to know, when they learn what is going on, what they can do. They feel alone and helpless. But we are not alone and we are not helpless. I have outlined a three-point program that can save this nation and the Constitution if the American people care enough to save it.

1. Begin by preparing yourself and your family to withstand an economic crisis. No matter how strong your love of the Constitution and the principles of freedom are today, if you see your family starving in a few weeks or months, you may be greatly tempted to sell the birthright of your American heritage of freedom for a mess of potage and accept the new constitution. Store a two-year supply of food and needed items for your family. Next, make sure you are living in a safe place where you can grow some food for your family. Have weapons and know how to use them; your life may depend upon it. If you live in a city with over a million people in it, you had better have a place to go at least two hundred miles away where you can live for a year or so until things begin to settle down. Finally keep as much of your financial assets in solid securities such as silver coins or bars, or food, or agricultural land. For more complete instructions see my book *How to Prepare for the Coming Crash.*

2. Spread the word. You have been warned; it is your duty to warn your neighbor. Do not argue with people. You

must not try to convince people against their will, regardless of who they are or how important they are to you. To try to force this message upon them will only make enemies of them and will not help them. But do everything you can to warn as many as you can about what is about to happen. Do not be concerned that there will be many who will not believe you and that some ignorant souls will attempt to ridicule you; the day and the hour is not far off when all will know that you spoke the truth.

3. Join with us in the Constitutional Party of America. This is a grass-roots organization of ordinary citizens. We have a three-fold plan. First is to organize for the purpose of becoming informed and informing others. Second is to be organized so that we can combine our individual power and strength in promoting men and women to public office at all levels who are dedicated to preserving and protecting the Constitution of the United States as given to us by our Founding Fathers and who will work to reverse the usurpation of our rights. Third is to provide a nucleus of dedicated citizens who will be trained to step into the vacuum of leadership that will be created when the national crisis occurs and will be able to mobilize the citizens of the nation along Constitutional lines to defend their rights, their property and their principles against all illegal usurpations from whatever source they might come. If you wish to join with me in this fight to preserve our Constitution, write to me, Robert L. Preston, Constitutional Party of America, P.O. Box 150, Provo, Utah 84601, and I will send you complete information.

But when a long train of abuses and usurpations, pursuing invariably the same Object evinces a design to reduce them under absolute Despotism, it is their right, it is their duty, to throw off such Government, and to provide new Guards for their future security. (Thomas Jefferson, *The Declaration of Independence*, July 4, 1776.)

What country can preserve its liberties, if its rulers are not warned from time to time, that this people preserve the spirit of resistance? (Thomas Jefferson, Nov. 13, 1778, *Works* 2:318.)

BIBLIOGRAPHY OF
THE PLOT TO REPLACE THE CONSTITUTION

Chapter One

1. p. 52, Vol. 3, No. 5, *The Center Magazine,* The Center for the Study of Democratic Institutions, Santa Barbara, California.
2. p. 13, Phillip Abbott Luce, *Road to Revolution.*
3. p. 14, Alice Widener, *Teachers of Destruction.*
4. p. 15, Luce, *op cit.*
5. p. 16, *Ibid.*
6. p. 52, Vol. 3 No. 5, *The Center Magazine.*
7. p. 52, *Ibid.*
8. p. 51, *Ibid.*
9. p. 51, *Ibid.*
10. p. 52, *Ibid.*
11. p. 1, *Ibid.*
12. Back Cover, Vol. 3, No. 6, *The Center Magazine.*
13. p. 8, Vol. 3 No. 5, *The Center Magazine.*
14. p. 9, *Ibid.*
15. *Ibid.*
16. p. 11, *Ibid.*
17. p. 9, *Ibid.*
18. p. 1, *Ibid.*

Chapter Two

1. January 9, 1956, *Newsweek.*
2. Nov. 19, 1949, *Report of The Study for the Ford Foundation on Policy and Programs.*
3. p. 89, Francis X. Gannon, *Biographical Dictionary of the Left.*
4. p. 946, Carroll Quigley, *Tragedy and Hope.*
5. p. 946, *Ibid.*
6. p. 62, Cleon Skousen, *The Naked Capitalist.*
7. pp. 50-51, Vol. 3 No. 5, *The Center Magazine.*
8. Robert Hutchins, *Encyclopedia Britannica, 1961 Year Book.*

9. p. 50, *The Center Magazine, op. cit.*

10. p. 163, Stuart Chase, *A New Deal.*

11. p. 272, Rose L. Martin, *Fabian Freeway.*

12. p. 273, *Ibid.*

13. p. 44, "Interlocking Subversion Report," Senate Internal Security Subcommittee, July 30, 1953.

14. p. 34, Ralph de Toledano, *Seeds of Treason.*

15. *Hearings,* House Select Committee to Investigate Certain Statements of Dr. William Wirt, 73rd Congress, 2nd Session, April 10 and 17, 1934.

16. *Ibid.*

Chapter Three

1. p. 11, Vol. 3 No. 5, *The Center Magazine.*

2. p. 14, *Ibid.*

3. *Ibid.*

4. Genesis 19:5.

5. Romans 1:26-27.

6. Turgeniev, Ivan, *Encyclopedia Britannica,* 1911.

Chapter Four

This entire chapter is taken from material published as *The Center Magazine,* Vol. 3, No. 5, Published by The Center for the Study of Democratic Institutions, Santa Barbara, California. This constitution is written in dry and difficult language and would be dull reading for most people, but for those serious scholars who would like to read this document for themselves they may order a reproduced copy from Freemen Institute, 839 North 700 East, Provo, Utah 84601. Be sure to send a dollar donation to cover costs.

ORDER BLANK

NAME _____

ADDRESS _____

CITY _____ STATE _____ ZIP _____

TITLE	Quantity	Price	Amount
"How To Prepare For The Coming Crash"	_____ X	_____	_____
"Wake-Up America"	_____ X	_____	_____
"The Plot To Replace The Constitution"	_____ X	_____	_____
		TOTAL	_____

┌─────────────────────────┐
│ ORDER SEVERAL   │
│ *********   │
│ Give to Friends and   │
│ Relatives — HELP   │
│ WAKE UP AMERICA   │
└─────────────────────────┘

1 thru 9 copies	2.00 each
10 thru 24 copies	1.80 "
25 thru 49 copies	1.70 "
50 thru 100 copies	1.60 "

Make checks payable and send your order to:

Wake-Up Publishing Co., P. O. Box 150, Provo, Utah 84601

Bookstores Contact Publisher - See Front of Book.